Blood Relative

ALSO BY MICHAEL ALLEGRETTO

Night of Reunion
The Dead of Winter
Blood Stone
Death on the Rocks

BLOOD

RELATIVE

Michael Allegretto

CHARLES SCRIBNER'S SONS
NEW YORK

MAXWELL MACMILLAN CANADA   TORONTO

MAXWELL MACMILLAN INTERNATIONAL
NEW YORK   OXFORD   SINGAPORE   SYDNEY

Copyright © 1992 by Michael Allegretto

Charles Scribner's Sons
Macmillan Publishing Company
866 Third Avenue
New York, NY 10022

Maxwell Macmillan Canada, Inc.
1200 Eglinton Avenue East
Suite 200
Don Mills, Ontario M3C 3N1

Macmillan Publishing Company is part of the Maxwell Communication Group of Companies.

Library of Congress Cataloging-in-Publication Data
Allegretto, Michael.
      Blood relative : a Jacob Lomax mystery / Michael
Allegretto.
            p.   cm.
      ISBN 0-684-19409-0
      I. Title.
PS3551.L385B65   1992
813'.54—dc20   91-39422
                                                         CIP

10 9 8 7 6 5 4 3 2 1

Printed in the United States of America

Dedicated to the memory
of Josephine Crigler.

Thanks to Jim Vander Laan and Susan Runkle for their kind assistance.

Blood Relative

CHAPTER

1

SAMUEL BUTLER HAD MURDERED HIS WIFE, and I was supposed to help him go free.

I didn't much like it. I preferred working for victims, not victimizers. And although Butler had yet to stand trial, everyone knew he was guilty. The cops, the district attorney, the media—they all knew it. It was hard not to agree with them. After all, you can't ignore the three M's.

These are—according to a boozy old cop I'd once ridden with—motive, means, and mother-jumpin' opportunity.

Butler had them all.

As I said, I didn't like it. But I needed the money.

I'd spent the past few months and the bulk of my savings in Puerto Vallarta in old Mexico, escaping the tag end of Denver's winter. I'd wasted my days on sunny beaches and my nights in cool bars, drinking tequila and Tecate and generally spreading goodwill, cheer, and *dinero* among our friendly neighbors to the south. Two neighbors in particular, a pair of lovely señoritas. Cousins, they were, with a house on a hillside overlooking the sea. And one of them had the most incredible way of . . .

. . . well, never mind.

Because here I was, seated in the oak-paneled, book-lined office of Oliver R. Westfall, attorney-at-law. I was tan but broke, wearing shoes and socks, not huaraches, and prepared to help free a murderer.

The calendar on Westfall's desk declared today April first. It seemed appropriate.

"Are you familiar with the details of this case, Mr. Lomax?"

"Just what I've seen on the nightly news."

"Yes, well, television."

Westfall was a small, quiet man. He wore dark blue slacks with faint stripes, a matching vest, and a blinding white shirt. His tie was maroon and subtly patterned. His suit coat was hung squarely on an oak valet in the corner. When he'd spoken to me, he'd shuffled papers on his desk, avoiding eye contact, as if he were embarrassed to be involved in this hopeless affair.

However, I was aware of Westfall's reputation in the courtroom. He was a tenacious fighter, worth every dollar of his fee. If you could afford him. Obviously, Samuel Butler could.

Now Westfall raised his eyes to me and smiled faintly. His large, round glasses and rosy cheeks made him look like a fifty-year-old little boy.

"Just so you know precisely where we stand," he said, "on Saturday, March sixteenth, at three-twenty in the afternoon, Samuel Butler called the police to his house. When they arrived, they found him distraught and smelling of alcohol. He said he'd just come home and found his wife Clare dead. She was sitting at the kitchen table, facedown, the back of her head crushed in, apparently by repeated blows from a blunt instrument. There were no signs that she had struggled or attempted to flee."

"So she wasn't alarmed by the presence of her assailant."

"Obviously." He spoke with confidence, as if he represented the prosecution, not the defense. "The subsequent investigation revealed no forced entry into the house. So she either admitted her assailant, or he had a key. In other words, she knew him."

"She was married to him."

Westfall gave me a sad look and folded his hands across his little vested belly. "Mr. Lomax, I wonder if you have the right attitude for this job."

"I'm sorry, I didn't mean to sound—"

He raised his hand and showed me his palm, a diminutive crossing guard telling the big kid to halt.

"The private investigator whom I usually employ was injured in an accident and is physically unable to work on this case," he said. "Otherwise you wouldn't even be here. You *are* here because you've been recommended by a colleague of mine. He said you'd be adequate for the task at hand."

"Only adequate?"

"For now, that's all I need. But I demand nothing less. Please try to remember that Samuel Butler is innocent until proven guilty."

"Of course."

My eyes moved past Westfall to the window and the square piece of building visible across Seventeenth Street, shimmering in the morning sun. I couldn't see the street far below. But I could picture the businessmen and businesswomen down there, dressed in business suits, bustling about in the chill spring air, with business on their minds. Business. I found myself drifting back to Mexico. While I'd been down there, I'd questioned whether I wanted to continue working as a private eye. Perhaps Westfall was right about my attitude.

I asked, "Do the police have any other suspects?"

"Unfortunately, no. After three days of investigation, they determined that Samuel Butler was the only one who could have murdered his wife. And the D.A. presented a convincing case to the grand jury:

"One, the police found the murder weapon, a heavy

crescent wrench belonging to Butler, hanging on a pegboard in the garage. It appeared to have been hastily
wiped with a rag, but lab technicians found Mr. Butler's
fingerprints at one end and traces of Clare Butler's blood,
hair, and scalp at the other. Two, before his arrest, Mr.
Butler admitted to police that that morning he'd argued
violently with his wife. Three, neighbors saw no one enter
or leave the Butler residence all day. Four, well, I think
you get the picture. Last Friday the grand jury returned
an indictment of first-degree murder. The judge ordered
Mr. Butler held without bond."

"No bond? But isn't he an established member of the
community? His family is here, his business . . ."

"Well, Mr. Butler has some history of violence. And
unfortunately, he made a vague but public threat to the
district attorney."

Big mistake. "What defense will you present?"

"That Samuel Butler was not home when his wife was
murdered. Of course, the D.A. won't argue this point.
He'll claim that Mr. Butler killed her, then left the house
for several hours, returned later, and called the police.
What I intend to show the jury is that during those hours
Samuel Butler was not behaving like a man who had just
committed murder."

I waited for more. "Is that it?"

"It may be enough to cast doubt in the minds of the
jurors. That's all I need to keep my client out of prison."

It seemed pretty thin to me. Of course, you have to
play the cards you're dealt.

"What do you want me to do?"

"Find four persons," Westfall said, "three of whom are
crucial for our defense. Mr. Butler spoke to these three
and no others while he was away from his house—while
his wife was being murdered. They can testify to his attitude and behavior."

"And the fourth person?"

4

"Mr. Butler can better explain about him," Westfall said. "As for the other three, I want them in here for depositions as quickly as possible. Memories fade."

"Do you have their names?"

"No."

Of course not. Otherwise he would've hired a process server, not an investigator.

Westfall explained that after Butler had left his house, he'd driven toward the mountains and stopped in Golden. He'd gone into the first bar he'd seen and sat in the company of two men. A few hours later, he'd walked unsteadily out to his car and driven home, along the way buying flowers for Clare.

"So you want the two guys in the bar and the person in the flower shop."

"Not a flower shop. A street vendor."

"Which intersection?"

"I don't know. Near his house, though."

"What's the name of the bar?"

"I don't know that, either. Mr. Butler said it was on the right-hand side as he drove into town."

"I'll need to talk to him."

"Of course. I'll arrange it. This morning, if you're prepared to start."

That was the question—was I prepared? I'd just returned from a fantasyland of warm days and soft nights, and part of my mind was still there. The rest of me was having trouble reentering the real world of work, bills, duties, and obligations. It was a little early for mid-life crisis—I'd be thirty-six this month—but I sure as hell was going through *something*.

"I'll need a recent photo of Butler," I said.

"I'm sure there's one at his house. You can get the key from my secretary on your way out."

Westfall opened a ledger-sized checkbook and inscribed my name and the amount we'd agreed on—my advance plus a week's per diem. If the job lasted longer or if I had any unforeseen expenses, we'd settle up later. Westfall would've preferred a contract, but fine print gives me a headache.

He carefully tore out the check and handed it to me. I had to stand to reach across his desk.

"Report the moment you locate these people," he said. "Time is of the essence." Then he began shuffling through some papers on his desk that had nothing to do with me. I was dismissed.

When I didn't leave, he looked up.

"Off the record," I said, "do you think Butler did it?"

Westfall's face remained impassive. But when he spoke, his voice expanded and hardened, like water freezing.

"Samuel Butler most definitely did *not* murder his wife."

He meant it.

Or maybe he was just rehearsing for the courtroom.

CHAPTER

2

THE DENVER COUNTY JAIL lies on the edge of an enormous open field just east of Stapleton International Airport.

I'd been there a number of times during my half-dozen years as a Denver cop, but not recently. There was a brand-new complex next door, the Reception and Diagnostic Center. If Samuel Butler were convicted of murder, he'd be transferred temporarily to the center, where he'd be studied and tested to see who his new roommates would be in the penitentiary in Cañon City—sort of a state-run dating service.

I passed through the razor-wire fences to the old jail buildings, showed my ID to a deputy sheriff, and was ushered through a couple of interior gates to a hallway.

Along the right-hand side were five enclosed booths, each with a pair of doors, windowed and numbered. Mine was "3."

The first booth was occupied by two black men, one in green, angry, the other in a suit, calm, if not bored. The second booth held two Hispanic men, with similar attire and attitudes.

I stood by my door and waited for Butler.

A few minutes later, he came toward me from the end of the hallway, accompanied by a deputy.

I'd never seen him before, but I knew at once it was Butler.

He was in his early fifties, a sturdily built man, about my weight, I'd guess, two hundred or less, and nearly as tall, perhaps six feet. He had black hair speckled with gray, shorter on the sides than on top, brushed straight back. His face was broad and ruddy. His thick black brows were slightly pinched together over the bridge of his nose, giving him a permanent scowl.

He didn't act frightened by his surroundings or familiar with them. He neither slouched nor strutted, but walked erect, with accustomed self-esteem—despite his baggy green jumpsuit. He stood out from the other jailbirds like a hawk among buzzards.

"Jacob Lomax?"

"Right."

He hesitated, studying me with displeasure. I knew he owned a company that employed dozens of workers. No doubt he'd fired a few in his time. This was the look he gave them just before the ax fell.

Finally, he jerked open his door. I opened mine, and we entered the booth and sat on our benches. A tabletop jutted out between us from the wall. We could've been sitting in a fifties diner. The deputy waited within shouting distance, ready to take our order.

"So. You're the detective." Butler's tone was condescending.

I nodded.

"Do you know Gil Lucero?" he asked suddenly.

"No."

"He's the private detective I've used in the past."

"Sorry, I've never heard of him."

"He's one of the best."

"Aren't we all."

Butler's scowl deepened, approaching anger. Then it

returned to merely annoyed. "Tell me why I should hire you?"

"Your attorney has already—"

"I pay his salary, too. Tell me why I should let you work for me."

"Shall I go home and fax you my résumé?"

Butler snorted, which may have been a laugh. Then he folded his thick hands on the tabletop. "I need you to find someone," he said.

"Your attorney said there were four, altogether."

"Forget what Oliver Westfall wants."

"He seemed to think three of them were crucial to—"

"*I'm* giving the orders here!" he shouted, making me wince. I hate it when people do that.

"I don't think so," I said evenly. "First, I may be working in your interest, but I'm working *for* Westfall. He's the one who signed my check. And second, it was my idea to come here. I can do this job with or without your cooperation." I paused, soaking up his glare. "Although," I said, "it'd be more efficient 'with.' "

He gripped the edge of the table so hard I expected metal to ooze between his fingers. His face was an ugly shade of red. I wondered if his family had a history of stroke. He took a couple of long, slow breaths. Gradually, his grip relaxed, and some of the color went out of his cheeks.

"All right," he said. His voice was strained, as if he would have preferred to shout. Who could blame him? He was staring at life in prison.

I got out a pad and pen.

"What time did you leave your house on the day of the murder."

"The police know all that."

"I'm not the police."

He pursed his lips, and his gaze moved up and to his left. "It was around ten-thirty in the morning."

"And then you drove straight to a bar in Golden?"

"That's where I ended up, but I don't know how 'straight' it was. See, Clare and I had had a terrible fight the night before, and we'd started up again that morning. We'd yelled at each other, said some terrible things. Things a husband and wife should never say to each other. I . . . I'd hit her."

For the first time, Butler's face registered something other than annoyance or anger. Pain. Perhaps sorrow.

"When I left the house, I wasn't thinking straight. I just wanted to get away, to drive. By the time I'd calmed down, I was on Sixth Avenue, heading west. I wanted a drink, and I was nearly to Golden." He moved his shoulders in a shrug.

"What was the name of the bar?"

"I didn't notice. I just parked and went in."

"Describe it."

Butler did. Golden was a small town, and I knew I'd find the saloon.

"Who'd you talk to in there?"

"The bartender. And some old guy named Winks."

Butler told me he'd sat at the bar, drinking whiskey shots and beer chasers. Before long he was crying in his booze, buying drinks for this character Winks, and spilling his guts out to him and the bartender. He told them how he'd mistreated his wife, how much he loved her, and how he feared losing her. They were both sympathetic; especially Winks, who had experienced several marriages and occasional domestic violence.

"What was the bartender's name?"

"I don't know."

"Describe him. Winks, too."

Butler did in detail.

"What time did you leave the bar?"

"I'm not sure. The police records show that I called

from my house at three-twenty that afternoon. So I mus-t've left Golden around two-thirty or so."

"Did you drive straight home?"

"I stopped to buy flowers. A peace offering."

"Where?"

"On Colorado Boulevard. Between the highway and Evans. Some kid was selling them in a parking lot. I bought all I could cradle in one arm, gave him a hundred-dollar bill, and told him to keep the change."

"He should remember you."

Butler nodded, his eyes a bit out of focus, remembering.

"When I got home, I was as nervous as a schoolboy on his first date, ready to do whatever was necessary to make up with Clare. And then I walked into the kitchen. . . ."

Again his face showed pain and sorrow. I didn't think he was faking it.

"She was slumped over the kitchen table in a pool of blood. The back of her head was . . . broken . . . smashed in. I . . . I could see . . . her *brain*. I . . ." He cleared his throat. "I didn't have to touch her to know she was dead. But when I did touch her, she was . . . so cold."

Slowly his expression changed. His eyes narrowed, and his jaw tightened. He stared hard at me, all signs of sorrow gone.

"Some son of a bitch killed her, Lomax, bashed in her head like a clay pot. She was mine, and he took her from me. And he's still out there somewhere."

I said nothing.

"The cops aren't even looking for him. I told the D.A. that if he didn't get who killed her, I'd beat *his* head. . . ." He heaved a sigh. "Everyone's so sure I did it. Other than Westfall, the only people who believe me are Kenneth, Karen, and Nicole—my children. Their love and support are keeping me from exploding in here." But-

MICHAEL ALLEGRETTO

ler licked his lips. "Being locked up, it's—I can barely
stand it. If I don't get out, I don't know . . . I might
really kill somebody."

I believed him.

"Don't worry, I'll find Mr. Winks and—"

"Forget about Winks. No, I don't mean that. Do what
Westfall wants. But find out who Clare was seeing."

"Seeing?"

"The fourth person you need to find is Clare's . . .
lover." Butler set his jaw and exhaled through his nose.
He hated talking about it. "Clare is—I mean, she was—
much younger than I am. I'd met her a few years after
my first wife died. Clare brought joy back into my life.
She was full of cheer, full of energy. After a while, well,
it was difficult for me to keep up with her. Sexually. She
took a lover. This was about four months ago. I found out
and put a stop to it.

"But she started up again recently. I didn't have any
proof, really, just an attitude change on her part. Preoccupied. Then, the night before she was killed, I overheard
her talking on the phone. Intimately. But angry, too, as
if she were having a lover's quarrel. She hung up when
she saw me standing in the doorway. She refused to talk
about it, and we fought. In the morning we fought some
more. . . ."

He fell silent. I waited.

"I told the police about Clare's first lover. I thought
she was seeing him again and that *he'd* killed her. They
questioned him, and he proved he'd been out of town at
the time of the murder. But I know she was seeing someone. If you can find him, at least the police will have
another *suspect*. Right now all they've got is me."

He had a mildly desperate look in his eyes, as if
he were hanging from a cliff by his fingers—and I
was standing over him.

"Why would your wife's lover kill her?"

12

"I—I don't know."

"Who was the first one, the man the police questioned?"

"I told you, he was out of town."

"Yes, but he might know things about Clare that you don't."

Butler winced at the thought. But he gave me the name: Christopher Pruitt.

"I'll need a recent photo of you," I said. I already had Westfall's permission and the key to Butler's house in my pocket, but I asked, anyway, "May I take one from your home?"

It was a small thing, a modicum of respect. It made Butler sit up a little straighter.

"Of course," he said. He told me where to find it. He also told me to speak to his son, who would help me in any way he could.

The interview was over.

We left the booth. The deputy led Butler away. Now that I'd met the man, I could see my first impression had been wrong. What I'd interpreted as confidence and self-esteem was merely self-control. Butler was straining to hold himself together.

And somehow I'd begun to doubt that he'd murdered his wife.

CHAPTER

3

I DROVE HOME TO GET A GUN.

When I'd left this morning, I'd believed the only killer I'd be dealing with was already locked up. But if Samuel Butler was innocent—and it seemed possible—then someone else had brutally murdered his wife. Someone I might bump into while I was nosing around. An altercation could ensue, and I wanted an appropriate response.

My home was just off Seventh Avenue, near the governor's residence. We both lived in mansions.

That is, my building had been constructed as a mansion around the turn of the century. Decades ago it was divided into eight apartments.

There were two apartments in the basement, one vacant, the other belonging to George. He unclogged drains, patched plaster, repaired leaks, and generally kept the grand old house from falling apart. I'm not sure how old he was. He still limped from a wound received in the Indian wars.

My wacky old landlady, Mrs. Finch, lived on the main level in what had long ago been her family's parlor and formal dining room.

The apartment across the hall from her was occupied by a continuous stream of tenants. Mrs. Finch kept renting and evicting, searching for just the right person to be on "her floor."

On the second floor, right below me, were my good friends Vassily and Sophia Botvinnov. They'd emigrated from Russia. Perhaps "escaped" might be a better word, since back then no one had heard of *glasnost*. Vaz was a grand master, retired now from world-class competition. He played chess the way Muhammad Ali had fought, smooth and powerful and nearly unbeatable. In fact, the only game I'd ever seen him lose was to an inferior player at a multiboard exhibition he'd given at a local chess club. When I questioned Vaz later about the loss, he told me, "Jacob, when a club sponsors me at an exhibition, I *always* lose to the treasurer, draw with the president, and beat everybody else."

Also on the second floor was a young couple I barely knew. They came and went a lot. Sophia called them "yoopies."

On the top floor was me and a vacancy. It had been that way since I'd moved in over three years ago. As far as I knew, Mrs. Finch had never tried to rent that apartment. She'd mentioned once that it had been the bedroom for her and her sisters, back when the place was still a mansion and her father was an affluent Denver merchant. Sometimes at night I'd hear her go in there and lock the door. She'd stay for hours.

I unlocked my door and went into my apartment.

Because the building had not been originally designed for multiple tenants, no two apartments were the same. You entered mine in the middle of the living room, with the kitchen to the left and the bed and bath through a doorway straight ahead. The apartment was probably the smallest in the building, but it had the best view, from a third-floor balcony off the eating area that overlooked the large backyard and the neighborhood to the east, north, and south. The view improved considerably in the summer when the secretaries in the apartment building across the alley worked on their tans beside the pool.

I passed through the living room to the bedroom. The bed was still unmade. Maybe the cleaning lady would make it. If I had a cleaning lady.

Out of respect for burglars, I kept the guns in the closet safe, a hundred-pound, two-foot cube. Presently, I owned two pieces: a nickel-finish .357 Magnum Colt Trooper and an Airweight Smith & Wesson .38 with a two-inch barrel.

I clipped on a hip holster with the smaller gun, then checked myself in the mirror. My jacket barely bulged. Jacob Lomax, armed and ready. The most dangerous man in the building, if not on the block.

But I hadn't worn a gun in months. It felt lumpy and awkward. And menacing, as if it would cause problems, not solve them. I considered taking it off.

While in Mexico I'd reflected on my six years as a cop, my four and a half years as a private snoop, and all the sociopaths who'd made it prudent for me to carry a gun— brawlers, backstabbers, and stone-cold killers. A never-ending stream of scum, mine for the wading. Why should I keep doing it?

Of course, there were the others, the ones who'd accidentally fallen into the stream or who'd been dragged in unwillingly. They'd needed someone to help them out. They'd always need someone.

But what made me think it had to be me?

I shut the safe and locked it. I kept the gun on.

The residence of Samuel and the late Clare Butler was on Adams Street, just north of Evans Avenue, a quiet, middle-class neighborhood. The house itself was a big, angular brick ranch, built in the late forties and painted off-white sometime later.

I parked in the driveway in the spiderweb shade of a giant weeping willow.

The next-door neighbor gave me the eye. He was short, fat, and balding, kneeling beside a flower bed of newly turned soil. He wore a white shirt, a blue cardigan sweater, baggy brown pants, and a pair of half-glasses. There was a trowel in his hand and a frown on his face.

He watched me go up the walk to Butler's front door. After I pulled open the screen and shoved the key in the lock, he called, "Hey."

He crossed the driveway and came up the walk toward me, stopping halfway.

"What do you think you're doing?" He pointed his trowel at me as if it were a sword.

"It's okay, I've got a key." I held it up for him to see.

He squinted.

"Samuel Butler's lawyer gave it to me," I said.

"His lawyer?"

I told him who I was and what I was doing. He lowered his weapon. He said his name was Pennypacker and that he'd lived in the house next door for thirty-seven years and that ever since he'd been burglarized five years ago, he'd kept a watchful eye for "suspicious-looking persons."

"Er, no offense."

"None taken," I said. "How well did you know Samuel and Clare?"

"Him, very well. I was here when he moved in with his first wife twenty, twenty-five years ago. She was a peach. Her name was May. A real sweet lady. I remember when she died." He clucked his tongue and shook his head.

"How did she die?"

"Brain tumor. It was sudden. Sam and the kids took it very hard. Before that, they'd been one big happy family. Then, a few years later, he took up with the other one."

"Clare."

He pursed his lips and nodded. "I knew *that* would never last. She was too young and wild for him. To tell you the truth, I'm not too surprised he killed her."

"Because she was wild?"

"Because they fought."

"I understand they had an argument the night before the murder."

"Argument is putting it mildly," he said. "I opened the back door to let in the dog, and I could hear them screaming bloody murder over there, calling each other names you wouldn't believe."

"Did you hear them fighting the next day?"

"The police asked me the same thing. No. The only thing I heard— Well, like I told them, it wasn't important."

"What?"

"I heard tires screech. It sounded as if it came from my driveway or Sam's. But when I looked out the window, there was no car, not even in the street."

"What time was this?"

Pennypacker shrugged. "Around noon, I think. Anyway, as I told the police, that night wasn't the first time I'd heard Sam and Clare fight. They'd had other yelling matches, one just a few months ago. That time, she ended up with a black eye and a mink coat."

"So he'd hit her and then buy her things?"

"Something like that. But don't start thinking Sam was a monster. I mean, he was a different man when he was married to his first wife, May. A good husband and a loving father, from what I could tell."

"So you think Clare changed him?"

"I do. She changed him into a murderer."

Pennypacker went back to his flower bed, and I went into the house.

The architect had been a freethinker, or else he'd mislaid his T square—the hallways and rooms were not quite at right angles.

I moved along the hallway to my right, sensing the emptiness of the house as a pressure in my ears, as if I were swimming underwater.

The living room had a hardwood floor and an enormous area rug with arcane designs in black and white. White leather couches and chairs were arranged for group conversation. A few black-steel, stick-thin lamps reached out from the corners like giant praying mantises.

I wandered into the kitchen, the scene of the crime.

It was large and airy. There was a table with four chairs, a big butcher block, and lots of counter space to accommodate the expensive, foreign-made small appliances. The tabletop gleamed, with not a trace of Clare Butler's blood.

I moved past it to a door and twisted open the dead bolt. An attached three-car garage. I was surprised—although I shouldn't have been—to find cars there: a two-year-old white Cadillac Seville and a new midnight-blue Porsche 911. I couldn't picture Butler driving a sports car, so I assumed the Porsche had belonged to Clare.

I stepped down into the garage.

There was a workbench along the rear wall, too clean and unblemished to have seen much use. The pegboard gleamed with hand tools, including three crescent wrenches. They were hung in a row according to length. The fourth hook was empty, apparently having once held the largest wrench, the murder weapon.

I went back into the kitchen and locked the door.

Westfall had told me Clare was bludgeoned while she sat at the table. I wondered if she'd sat with her back to this door or if the killer had had to walk around her, hiding the wrench at his side. Either way, she hadn't been alarmed by his presence.

I moved toward the living room and veered right, through a wide doorway, into the sunroom.

Wicker furniture with pastel cushions was arranged about the stone floor. The room had once been a patio. Large windows opened onto the sprawling backyard.

There were plenty of leafless trees out there, some just budding, and a few stately evergreens. The flower beds were beginning to bloom with perennials. Near the rear of the yard, a hundred feet from the house, a gazebo was being swarmed by thick, leafless vines.

I turned to the wall behind me, which was hung with family photographs. Butler had told me to look here for a suitable picture.

However, most of the photos showed him as a much younger man, with his first wife and their three children—a son and a daughter about a year apart and a cute, chubby little girl who'd come along six or seven years later. The only recent pictures of Butler were snapshot-sized, with him wedged in among his children.

I wanted something more close up.

I found it in the master bedroom. On the bureau was a silver-framed head-and-chest picture of Butler and a young woman, young enough to be another daughter. Clare. She was extremely attractive, almost professionally so, with stylish blond hair, violet eyes, and a generous mouth. Both she and Butler wore sweaters with turtlenecks underneath. She looked like an advertisement for a ski resort. Butler looked brutish beside her. I slipped the photo from its frame.

Before I left the room, I made a brief search of the closets. Not because I was looking for anything in particular. Just professional nosiness.

The closets were his-and-hers walk-ins, each a small room. Butler's was only about half full. There were shelves for sweaters and a rack for shoes. His shirts were mostly solid colors—off-white and pale blue. He had half a dozen sports coats and fewer suits, not much for a guy with money. There was one Armani that stood out like a

First Communion suit in a kid's closet. I wondered if Clare had made him buy it.

I was certain she had when I stepped into her closet.

It looked like a boutique. Dozens of sweaters and twin racks jammed with dresses, blouses, pants, and jackets—everything with designer labels, some unworn, still with price tags attached. I pulled open the built-in drawers. Each was filled with silk undergarments.

Then something shiny caught my eye, tucked between the side of the drawer and a black silk negligee. I turned it over in my fingers.

It was a short, clear glass tube—a fluted mouthpiece at one end and a hollow ball at the other, with a tiny hole on top of the ball—some kind of pipe. I doubted that you could smoke hash in it. And it wasn't like any crack pipe I'd ever seen. But it definitely had the look of drug paraphernalia.

I sniffed it. Odorless.

Had Clare been into drugs? If so, I wondered if they'd had anything to do with her murder.

I put the pipe in my pocket and left the house, locking the front door behind me.

Then I climbed into the Olds and headed toward the mountains.

21

CHAPTER

4

IT DIDN'T TAKE LONG to get to Golden, which lies in the folds of the foothills west of Denver.

I hadn't been there since early last fall—also because of someone's death. Then the area had been brown and dry, baking under the last of summer's heat. Now it was brown and wet, with large patches of white. The shady mountainsides would show snow for at least another month.

I cruised down the main drag between one- and two-story storefronts, some new, some as old as the century. There were pedestrians moving about on the wide sidewalks. Few business suits. Mostly blue jeans and jackets or sweaters. I could smell hops being brewed into Coors beer a few blocks away.

Then I spotted the bar Butler had described to me.

As he'd said, it was on the corner, the bar entrance in front, the one to the restaurant on the side, a theater across the street. Another Rambo movie. Doesn't that guy know when to quit?

I nosed the Olds against the curb between a pair of pickup trucks, one of which sat high atop huge muddy tires. Each vehicle had a gun rack in the rear window.

The inside of the establishment also fit Butler's description.

It was as dim as a saloon should be at eleven-thirty in the morning. A bar stretched down the right side, fronted by a dozen four-legged wooden stools. The mirror on the wall doubled an uneven row of liquor bottles. The left side of the room was crowded with empty tables. Farther up on the left was a large open doorway. I could hear the faint clack of pool balls.

A waitress with yellow hair and a peasant blouse came through the doorway carrying a tray of empty beer bottles. She unloaded them on the bar and said, "Four more."

I took a stool and waited while the bartender popped open some cold bottles and the waitress toted them back through the doorway.

He asked me, "What'll it be?"

There was little doubt that this was Butler's bartender. He was around thirty, average looking in nearly all respects—medium height and weight, medium brown hair and eyes. His mustache, though, was uncommon. It was as thick as a brush and completely covered his mouth. The ends were longer still, waxed and twisted tightly into six-inch spikes that pointed straight out at each side. His wife wore safety goggles.

I let him draw me a beer. Then I showed him the picture of the Butlers.

"Do you recognize the man?"

He frowned at the picture. "I'm not sure. Who is he?"

"Samuel Butler. He said he was in here two weeks ago last Saturday drinking shots and beers with a guy named Winks."

His eyes brightened. He may have even smiled behind his hairy muzzle. "Sure, I remember him now. Coors and Wild Turkey. Winks probably had the same. It's what he does when someone else is buying."

"What time did Butler come in?"

He frowned briefly. "Are you a cop or something?"

"Private detective."

"Wait a sec."

The waitress had returned with some bills. The bartender rang up the sale and gave her change, which she dropped in her bank, a cocktail glass. He came back to me and raised his eyebrows.

"You asked?"

"The time Butler came in."

"I can't say for sure. Except it must've been before noon, because I remember it was slow, and we always get people in here for lunch, even on Saturdays."

"How did Butler act?"

"Act? I don't know. He sat about where you're sitting and had a drink or two alone before Winks drifted over and joined him. He's good at that. Winks, I mean."

"Did you hear them talking?"

"Not really."

"How long was Butler here?"

He shook his head, slicing the air with the sharpened points of his mustache.

"No idea. We got busy, and I think he and Winks moved into the back room. I didn't see him leave the bar."

I nodded, getting out my pad and pen. "I appreciate your help," I said, then asked for his name, address, and phone number.

"Why?" He was thinking, *hassle*.

"Butler's attorney wants to see you. It's no big deal." I didn't tell him he'd probably use up half a day driving to Denver and back and answering questions in front of a stenographer.

He said, "Shit," but he told me his name, Randy Stilwell, and where he lived.

"What's Mr. Winks's first name?"

"Beats me," he said. "Everyone calls him Winks."

"Where can I find him?"

Stilwell shrugged. "He comes in here a couple times a week."

"Where does he live?"

"I don't know. Up in the hills somewhere."

"Elliot could probably tell you." The waitress had spoken from the end of the bar. Stilwell and I turned to look at her. "If he's not too drunk already," she said. "He's in the back room shooting pool."

This private-eye business was easier than I remembered. I nodded my thanks and picked up my glass of beer.

The "back room" could seat a hundred or two.

Against the distant wall, to my right, was a battered wooden bandstand. There were microphones on chrome stands, huge mute speakers, and an elaborate, silent set of drums. A cowboy boot was sketched in glitter on the face of the bass drum. The scuffed and barren hardwood dance floor was rimmed by wooden tables and metal folding chairs. More tables were crowded into the rear half— the near half—of the room. There was enough space behind the last seats for a pair of coin-operated pool tables.

Dead animals overlooked it all.

Mounted high on the walls were the heads of deer, antelope, elk, and mountain cats. A few stuffed pheasants had been thrown in for color. On Friday nights amplified noise would rattle their glass eyes.

I wondered if the two guys shooting pool were responsible for any of the mounted heads.

They were in their early thirties, one big, one small, dressed alike—blue jeans, plaid flannel shirts, and rough-cut boots. The big guy had a full red beard. He sat with one haunch on a table beside a group of beer bottles. He selected one and took a long pull. When he spoke, his voice boomed.

"Elliot, you are one lucky son of a bitch."

"Hey, that's the way I planned it."

I walked in. They looked me over—sports coat, slacks, no tie—figured that I was neither friend nor foe, and returned their attention to the table.

Elliot picked up a small blue cube and chalked his cue, grinning like a smart ass. He had an angular face, a pointed Adam's apple, and a lot of brown curly hair piled on top of his head. A bunch of keys jangled at his side. When he spoke, he slurred a few words.

"What I did was," he explained to his big red bearded pal, "I used left English on that shot, just like I saw a guy do on TV. It's all angles, anyway, like geometry."

"Jesus Christ." Big Red turned toward me and shook his head sadly. "You see what I have to put up with?"

I gave him a shrug, then said to Elliot, "Are you Elliot?"

He moved around the table and began lining up the game-winning shot—eight ball in the corner. "Who wants to know?"

"My name is Lomax. I don't mean to interrupt your game, but I—"

"But you *are* interrupting it," Elliot said, grinning up at his pal. "Right?"

Big Red shrugged at me.

"Plus you're in my way," Elliot said.

I gave him a grin that made him look twice. Then I said, "Sorry," and moved away from the end of the table.

Elliot hunched over, set his narrow jaw in concentration, and fired. He sank the eight, but he'd shot much too hard. The cue ball banked off the end cushion, rolled all the way back toward him, and dropped in the corner pocket. Big Red boomed a laugh.

"God *damn* it."

"Tough break," I said. Then, "I was told you could tell me where to find a man named Winks."

"So what." Elliot began fishing quarters out of his jeans.

"So where can I find him?"

"What do you want with Winks?" Big Red asked me.

"He's going to testify at a murder trial."

Elliot gave me an incredulous look.

"*Winks?*"

I nodded. "My client's lawyer wants very much to talk to him."

Elliot said, "Winks on the witness stand? Can we watch?" Then he laughed at his own joke. Big Red chuckled.

"Is there something wrong with Mr. Winks?"

Elliot put quarters in the change taker, shoved it in, and pulled it out. Pool balls rumbled and clicked under the end of the table.

"First of all, there's no 'mister' to him." Elliot squatted down and slapped a plastic triangle onto the stained green felt. "His real name is Russ Armbruster. They call him Winks because he's got this thing with his eye."

"Where can I find him?"

"And *second* of all, he's about as loony as they come."

"Nice way to talk about your neighbor," Big Red put in.

"Neighbor, shit." Elliot began plunking balls into the triangular rack. He paused, looked up at me, and explained, "Winks owns the acreage to the south of mine. If I'd've known about him, I never would've moved there. He likes to shoot at aliens."

"Illegal aliens?"

"Aliens from outer space," Big Red said, and chuckled into his beard.

I looked at Elliot for confirmation. He nodded.

"Winks is fairly certain that *they* have landed and live among us. He claims they look just like people except for a glow around them that only he can see."

Terrific. Samuel Butler's fate depended on a guy who was trying to kill E.T.

27

"Can you tell me how to get to his place?"

"I can show you." He checked his watch. "As soon as I whip this big bastard in one more game."

Big Red said, "In your dreams."

The "one game" turned into three. I had time to order a sandwich from the bar. Meanwhile, Elliot and friend slammed down beers as if aliens really had arrived. I learned that they were both welders at Rocky Flats, midnight to eight, disassembling contaminated glove boxes. I guess I'd drink like that, too, if my job description included the word "plutonium."

We left the bar at one, which was about ten o'clock their time. The bright sunlight made us all blink. Big Red climbed into his pickup and drove away. Elliot's was the other one, the one with the giant muddy tires.

"How, ah, tough is it to get where we're going?"

He grinned at the old Olds. "It'll be a challenge," he said.

CHAPTER

5

I FOLLOWED ELLIOT'S TRUCK NORTH out of Golden. He drove fairly straight for a guy who'd been drinking beer for the past five hours.

The residential street quickly transformed into a two-lane highway. There were low brown hills to the left and open brown plains to the right. We turned left at a sign marked Golden Gate Canyon Road.

Soon we were snaking through piny hillsides, splotched white with old snow. Elliot's truck slowed, then angled off the asphalt onto an ill-maintained road. The Olds thudded and creaked arthritically over rocky bumps and muddy potholes. The truck's brake lights went on. I stopped. Elliot's arm pointed out his window. I saw a narrow, rocky space between the evergreens. I assumed it was a road.

Elliot waved once, then spun his macho tires, tossed gravel onto my hood, and disappeared around a curve.

I eased the Olds to the left and set her crawling through the trees. I held the wheel with both hands to fight the violent contours of the trail. It twisted steadily upward. A few miles later, the road flattened, and the trees opened.

The residence sat at the rear of a straw-colored meadow. Either Winks had a big family, or carpentry was his hobby. Unpainted, weathered wings sprouted one

from the other at each end of the house. An addition
to the farthest right-hand wing was under construction.
Skeletal two-by-fours shone in the sun like the bones of
a prehistoric beast.

Three other beasts, live ones, charged across the
meadow toward me.

They were shaggy mongrels—small but territorial. They
surrounded the Olds. I rolled up the window to shut out
their piercing, vicious little barks.

I drove slowly forward. The trail skirted the meadow
and approached the house from the side, taking me past
a pile of rusted, twisted metal, perhaps the wreckage of
a UFO. I stopped the car near the house and shut off the
engine.

The only sound was the muted yapping of the munchkin-sized monsters.

A man came around the rear of the house. He was in
his sixties, with a few days' growth of white stubbly beard.
He wore baggy blue jeans, scruffy boots, a blue cotton
shirt, and a red down vest. A green cap that said John
Deere was pulled down hard on his head.

I inferred from his shotgun that he was cautious about
strangers.

He carried the weapon at port arms and walked up to
my side of the car. I rolled down the window and tried
to say, "Howdy," but his yapping dogs drowned me out.
He kicked at one of them, and they all shut up. I noticed
he was winking at me, his right eye twitching
uncontrollably.

"Are you from the assessor's office?" he demanded in a
crusty voice.

"No, sir." Always call a man with a shotgun "sir."

"Then what the hell do you want here?" Wink, wink.
"This is private property."

"Sir, my name is Jacob Lomax. I'm looking for Russ

Armbruster. Elliot said I could find him here. Are you Mr. Armbruster?" Of course he was. Winks.

"How do you know Elliot?"

"I just had a beer with him at a bar in Golden."

Winks snorted and winked. "A beer. Elliot seldom stops at one."

I smiled pleasantly. He was still holding the shotgun, although more loosely now.

"I'm a private detective working for Samuel Butler's attorney."

He frowned. "Butler. The name sounds familiar."

I showed him the photograph. "He said he drank with you in Golden two weeks ago last Saturday."

"Sure," he said, smiling, winking at the photo. "I remember him. Hell of a nice guy." His smile faded. "You said 'attorney.' Is he in trouble?"

"Mr. Butler's been charged with murdering his wife."

He stared at the photo of Samuel and Clare. "Her? I'll be goddamned." He shook his head and winked. "You know, that's about all that poor son of a bitch wanted to talk about."

"What, killing his wife?"

"Hell no. How much he loved her."

"Can we go in the house and talk?"

The kitchen was dirty but tidy. There was a greasy gas range, a smudged white refrigerator, and worn wooden cabinets. Cans of flour, sugar, and coffee were carefully lined up on the linoleum countertop. Recently washed dishes sat in the drainer, drying, and a moldy dishrag hung neatly over the faucet. The floor was gritty underfoot.

We sat on wooden chairs at the chipped, white-painted table. The dogs settled at our feet.

Winks poured us coffee in mugs. He added Jack Daniel's to his, then raised his eyebrows to ask me if I wanted some. His right eye continued to twitch. It was starting to get on my nerves. But at least he'd put away his gun.

"Sure," I told him.

He poured in a shot and asked, "Did he shoot her?"

"No, she was bludgeoned with a wrench."

Winks tucked in his chin and leaned away from me, as if I'd just told him that Clare Butler had been trampled to death by mice.

"Bludgeoned?"

"That's what the police say."

Winks shook his head, winking. "That surprises me more than him killing her."

"Why?"

"Because I figured he was sorta like me."

"Meaning what?"

"Meaning if he was gonna kill his wife, he'd use something designed and built for the purpose. Not a *wrench*."

I sipped my bourbon-laced coffee and thought this over. It was a weak point—the choice of murder weapon. I doubted Oliver Westfall could use it. But then, you never know about lawyers.

"You said you and Butler talked about his wife."

"Mostly he talked."

"What did he say?"

Winks drank from his mug, then poured in another slug of bourbon.

"He loved her, he needed her, he wanted her," Winks said in a singsong voice. "All that kinda crap." He drank his coffee-flavored bourbon and winked. "Listen, I had a couple of wives myself, and I know how they can twist your mind around so you start thinking that your life wouldn't be worth a damn without them. Hell, they *invented* marriage, men didn't." He drank from his mug and poured in more bourbon. "You ever been married?"

"Yes."

"Then you know what I'm talking about. Me, now, I'm

finished with women. Besides, how can you trust any of them since the landings."

"The what?"

He squinted at me, winking. "Never mind," he said.

Oh, the *landings*. I asked him, "Did Butler talk as if his wife were still alive?"

Winks winked. "That's a damn fool question. Course he did. He talked about how they'd fought and he'd hit her and he was afraid she would leave him. I almost told him 'good riddance,' but I could see he was hurting. So I gave him the secret of getting a woman to forgive you."

He paused and forced me to ask, "And what might that be?"

"Flowers." He winked. "Works every time."

"I see." So the flowers had been Winks's idea. "Then what?"

Winks shrugged, winking. "After that he seemed happier, I guess. We had a few more rounds, and then he was anxious to get home to . . . the *wife*." Winks made it sound unmanly.

"What time did he leave?"

"Well, I stayed on till three, like I usually do. And he'd left a bit before that. Say, two-thirty."

This confirmed what Butler had told me. And what Westfall had implied, that Butler wasn't behaving like a man who'd just killed his wife. Westfall would no doubt tell the jury that if Butler were trying to establish a phony alibi, he certainly would've done something more reliable than drive to Golden and drink with a total stranger, a semireclusive flake.

Although the flake part could be a problem. Winks might not volunteer a deposition for Westfall. And when he did appear on the witness stand, either by his own volition or under order of subpoena, the D.A. might get him talking about aliens.

Of course, this was assuming Winks would come to

court peaceably and not shoot the process server. Who, come to think of it, would probably be me.

I thanked Winks for his hospitality and drove back toward Denver.

CHAPTER

6

IT WAS ONLY THREE O'CLOCK, and already I'd put about a hundred miles on the Olds driving from downtown to the county jail to southeast Denver to Golden and beyond, finding Butler's bartender and Winks. A full day's work by anyone's measure. Now I could find a bar and take the rest of the day off.

Except it was too early to start drinking.

Hell, I could just go home.

And do what, housework? Maybe I needed a hobby. Or a pet, something to fill my spare time. Or maybe I'd been living alone too long.

Quit whining, Lomax, and get busy.

As I came out of the hills on Sixth Avenue, the eastern sky spread before me, hazy blue turning to smog brown near the horizon. There was an inversion layer today, warmer air above, cooler air below, trapping the pollution at ground level. The tallest downtown buildings stood like waders, hip-deep in muddy waters.

I cursed the pollution and steered my fossil-fueled machine south on I-25.

This was the route Samuel Butler had taken the day Clare was murdered. He'd bought flowers on his way home, a peace offering.

Or was it just part of his phony alibi?

After all, the evidence weighed heavily against Butler. Even I'd believed he was guilty after talking to his attorney. Why was I so sure now that he was innocent? Maybe I was kidding myself. Maybe I simply *wanted* him to be innocent so that I'd feel I was working on the side of justice.

I took the turnoff at southbound Colorado Boulevard.

It was about a quarter mile to Evans Avenue. In between was a La Quinta Motor Inn, a Perkins, and a Denny's. There were no flower vendors in sight. It was three o'clock now, perhaps too early for them. Or maybe they only worked the area on weekends.

In either case I'd have to come back later.

In the meantime, I could start looking for Clare Butler's secret lover.

I headed toward Englewood, Denver's immediate suburb to the south.

It's mostly residential, low-income and lower-middle-income families living in one-story frame or brick houses. The area I wanted, though, was the least attractive part of town—warehouses, auto graveyards, and shabby trailer parks. The sewage plant is well within smelling distance. Today it lent the air the faintest of odors. Enough, though, to ruin your appetite.

I turned off Dartmouth Avenue into a crowded parking lot that stretched before a building the size of an airplane hangar. A big semi turned in after me. Its trailer was painted with the logo of a regional trucking outfit. It rumbled around the side of the building past a sign that read Pickup and Deliveries in the Rear.

I'd heard that twenty years ago, when Samuel Butler had been a truck driver, he'd glued a small Peterbilt emblem onto his belt buckle, just for show. His fellow truckers thought that looked pretty damn good. They all wanted buckles like that. So did their friends. And friends of friends. Before long, Butler was so busy gluing emblems onto belt buckles and watch fobs and cigarette lighters that he'd had to quit his trucking job.

Today Butler Manufacturing Company still affixed company logos to cheap jewelry and personal accessories. But its yearly sales were a few million bucks.

I pushed through the building's glass front door.

A wide, well-traveled, carpeted hallway ran straight back to a door marked Employees Only. Beside the door was a gray-metal time clock with about three dozen cards in their slots.

To my right was another door that looked more inviting. It was open, anyway.

Beyond the door were four women—two young, two middle-aged—seated at big metal desks, two on each side, forming an aisle to a pair of doors in back. The desk tops were cluttered with file folders and loose papers. The younger women were typing up orders. The older two were on the phone, talking to customers. There were gray-metal filing cabinets lined up against one wall and a hat rack hung with jackets.

The air was too warm, and the fluorescent lights hummed overhead.

No one paid me any attention. I guess Butler Manufacturing didn't get much walk-in trade.

Finally, one of the women hung up her phone and asked, "Can I help you?" in a tone somewhere between boredom and annoyance.

She was fiftyish, with short dyed-black hair and pink button earrings. A pink cardigan sweater was draped over her shoulders, and a gold-toned chain dangled from the frames of her glasses and around the back of her neck.

"I'm here to see Kenneth Butler."

"And you are?"

"Jacob Lomax."

"With?"

"Excuse me?"

She rolled her eyes. "With what company?"

"I'm working for Samuel Butler's attorney."

Now they all looked at me.

"Just a moment." The woman pushed a button on her phone, announced me, listened, then said, "Go ahead on back."

The door on the left opened before I got there. It was obvious that the man in the doorway was Kenneth Butler. He looked just like his father, only shorter. A newer, economy-sized model.

He was around thirty, sturdily built, with a wide face. Like his father, he brushed his hair straight back, longer on top than the sides. His thick black eyebrows were pinched together, giving him a permanent scowl, though perhaps not as severe as his father's. His clothes were a bit more upscale than what I'd seen in the old man's closet—tailored gray slacks, blue pin-striped shirt with a white collar, and a fashionable tie. There were tassels on his shiny black loafers.

He grunted for me to come in and didn't offer to shake hands. A chip off the old block.

The office was windowless, with a door in the right-hand wall, leading, I supposed, into Daddy's office. Kenneth motioned me into one of the two visitors' chairs, then sat behind his desk.

The desk was old enough to need stripping and refinishing. A wobbly bookcase leaned against the near wall, ready to collapse under the weight of catalogs and price books. The walls were covered with cheap paneling and dusty display cards of belt buckles, earrings, lapel pins, lighters, pen-and-pencil sets, and so on—each tagged with a different company logo. Obviously, the Butlers didn't waste money on office amenities. But then, most of their business was probably done by telephone and delivery.

Kenneth started to speak, then seemed startled by the open ledger book before him. He quickly closed it and shoved it in a desk drawer, as if he were afraid I might steal some grave company secret, like how many lapel pins they'd sold last week.

"I thought you'd call first," he said.

"Oh? Were you expecting me?"

"Oliver Westfall phoned me at noon. He said my father wants me to help you in any way I can."

"You don't sound too happy about it."

"Why should I be? There's nothing *I* can do. It's a matter for the courts now." He made it sound like a law of nature.

"There may be a few stones yet unturned," I said.

"Meaning what?"

"Oliver Westfall and I are operating under the assumption that your father is innocent."

"Of course. That's your job."

I wondered if that's all it was.

"Speaking of that," he said, "have you found the men my father says he was with on the day he— On that day?"

"Two out of three. The bartender and the other man in the bar. I'm still looking for the flower vendor. And Clare's lover."

"Her *lover*?"

"Your father believed she was having an affair. If she was, I intend to find out with whom."

Kenneth looked peeved. "What difference does it make now? And how would I know anything about that?"

Only now did it occur to me that Clare Butler had been younger than Kenneth. That must have made for some awkward moments during family get-togethers.

"To answer your second question first," I said, "I have no idea what you can tell me about . . . your stepmother."

He winced, ever so slightly.

"But I have to start someplace," I said. "And after all, she was your stepmother."

"I'd prefer that you didn't use that term."

39

"Sorry." I wasn't. There was something I didn't like about Kenneth. Maybe it was his shiny shoes and his shabby office. Or his too cool attitude about his father facing life in prison. "As to your first question, it could make all the difference in the world if your—if Clare were having an affair. In fact, her lover may have murdered her."

He grimaced and shook his head. "My father's desperate theory."

"You don't agree?"

"Of course not. And digging up dirt about that woman will only cause our family more pain and humiliation. Face it, my father kil—"

He stopped himself and looked down at his hands. They were clenched together, fingers intertwined, as if he were afraid to let go, afraid of what might happen. Then he sighed and sagged in his chair.

"I wish it weren't so," he said sadly. "I love my father. We all do, my sisters and I. He's given us . . . so much. But we'll have to learn to live with this tragedy." He looked up at me with pain in his eyes. "All we can hope for," he said, "is a compassionate judge and jury."

"Right. By the way, where were you the day Clare was murdered?"

"I was—" His sad look turned to a glower. "What the hell are you implying?"

"Nothing. I'm just being thorough. As your father requested."

"*He* knows where I was. I was home all day with my wife, Doreen. You can ask her."

I intended to. "Let's talk about Clare."

He glared at me a moment longer. Then he looked away and shook his head, a sour expression on his face. "My sister Karen is who you should talk to. She's known Clare longer than anyone has, even my father. Although there was no love lost between her and Clare."

"Why?"

"Clare met my father through Karen," he said flatly, as if that explained it.

"Where can I find Karen?"

He gave me her home and business numbers. Then he said, "Don't be disappointed if she can't help you find Clare's lover. Because if Clare *had* a lover, the person who'd know all the details would be my father. He watched her like a hawk."

"Perhaps," I said, "but sometimes the last person to know is the husband."

Kenneth frowned, as if he were worrying about his own wife.

I asked him, "Was your wife friendly with Clare?"

He snorted. "Hardly. As far as I know, Clare didn't have any friends."

"There must've been someone."

"No one I knew about."

"I see. Do you know if Clare did drugs?"

"What? No, I'm sure she didn't. My father would never stand for that."

I took out the little glass pipe I'd found in Clare's drawer and set it on Kenneth's desk. He scowled at it.

"It belonged to Clare."

He shrugged. "What is it?"

His intercom buzzed before I could answer. He pressed a button and said, "Yes, Alice."

"Wes is here."

Kenneth asked me, "Was there anything else you wanted from me?"

"Not at the moment."

He glowered to show me he wouldn't appreciate being bothered in the future. Then he said, "You might as well meet Wes Hartman. He's one of the family, married to my little sister."

"Karen?"

"Nicole." He told Alice to send Wes in.

A moment later, there was a quick knock on the door behind me, and Wes Hartman entered the room. I stood, and Kenneth introduced us.

Hartman was a few years younger than Kenneth, with a wiry build, sandy hair, and too many teeth in his smile. He wore designer jeans, a forest-green suede jacket, over-priced running shoes, and aviator shades on top of his head. His stainless-steel watch told him the time in six major cities.

"Glad to meet you," he said. He gave my hand a hard squeeze to show me that he worked out. I tried not to scream in pain. He asked, "How are things progressing with Sam's defense?"

"Slowly."

He made a clucking sound and put on an appropriately somber expression. "What a tragedy," he said. "For everyone. It's a credit to Kenneth that the company's running so smoothly in his father's absence."

We were still standing, and Kenneth shuffled uncomfortably from one foot to the other.

I asked Hartman, "Do you work here?"

"Yes."

"May I ask in what capacity?"

"I'm in sales."

Oh, big surprise. "How well did you know Clare?"

"So-so," he said, then smiled. "Say, you guys really get to the point in a hurry, don't you?"

"We guys?"

"Private eyes." He chucked me on the shoulder with his fist. "Look, maybe we can do lunch sometime. But I need to talk business with Kenny right now, before I go see a new client. I'm sure you understand."

"Of course. Business before pleasure."

Hartman's brow wrinkled, as if he weren't sure what I meant.

"Perhaps I could stop by your home tonight," I suggested. "I'd like to ask you and your wife a few questions."

"Nicole? Well . . . she hasn't been feeling well. This whole affair has been devastating for her."

"I can appreciate that. I'll speak in hushed tones."

"Excuse me?"

"What time should I come over?"

He was still frowning at "hushed tones."

"Tonight's out of the question," he said, annoyed.

"Tomorrow night, then."

"Call first."

"No problem." I turned to Kenneth. "I'll talk to you soon." I picked up the glass pipe from his desk. Wes Hartman stared at it. I asked him, "Do you know what this is?"

"I've never seen it before in my life."

"I didn't say you had."

He hesitated; then one corner of his mouth curled up. He took the pipe from me and casually held it with his thumb and two fingers. "Some sort of pipe, isn't it?" He handed it back. "Is it yours?"

"It is now." I said good-bye and left them to their legitimate business.

But I'd gotten the impression that Wes Hartman was familiar with little glass pipes.

CHAPTER

7

I SAT IN THE OLDS and waited for Hartman. I wanted to ask him about Clare Butler and the glass pipe—out of the presence of his brother-in-law.

Hartman came out twenty minutes later. I walked across the lot toward him, but he climbed into his car, which he'd left in a no-parking zone by the front door, and sped away before I got halfway there.

I hurried back to the Olds and drove after him.

It bothered me that I hadn't noticed his car when I'd left the building. It would've been hard for *anyone* to miss, let alone an ace private eye—a blood-red Nissan 300 ZX, about forty thousand dollars' worth of personal transportation. Mexico had definitely blurred me.

Hartman went east on Dartmouth, then north on Santa Fe, heading toward downtown Denver. It seemed silly for me to honk and get his attention to pull over, so I just stayed a few cars behind him. Maybe I'd follow him for a while, get back in practice.

I was wondering, though, how a guy who sold junk jewelry could afford a 300 ZX. Of course, being married to the boss's daughter was always a plus.

Before we'd gone far, I saw Hartman use his car phone. Big shot.

Hell, *I'd* had a car phone. For a while, anyway. Before

Mexico I'd been on a case that necessitated having one of those high-tech toys installed. But then I'd purposely crashed the Olds into the rear of another car, and the toy had broken. A few other things had broken as well. In fact, after considerable repairs to restore her body to 1958 showroom perfection, the old girl still pulled a bit to her left. But at least she wasn't flaunting a telephone, for chrissake.

Hartman got on the freeway northbound and exited several miles later onto Speer Boulevard, heading away from the center of town. He swung over to Twenty-ninth Avenue and angled back toward downtown on Fifteenth Street.

The street ran downhill toward the Platte River and the railroad yards and beyond to the steel-and-glass skyscrapers. Not many years ago the old brick buildings along here had housed a few art galleries and Muddy's coffeehouse, gathering places for the new bohemians. Then came the real estate speculators, buying up the buildings and chasing out the low-income crowd with sky-high rents. The greedy folks had counted on renovations bringing in yuppies. What they hadn't counted on was a crash in the real estate market.

Now most of the buildings stood vacant.

There was one business, though, that had thus far weathered all storms—My Brother's Bar. It sat between the freeway and the river, signless, an unassuming brown exterior. The interior featured great burgers, imported beers on tap, and taped classical music.

Hartman parked on the corner near the entrance.

This must be where he was meeting the "new client" he'd mentioned to Kenneth Butler.

The street was fairly deserted—much too late for the lunch crowd and too early for the after-work drinkers. So when Hartman climbed out of his car, he saw me drive up.

He waved, looking surprised—and apprehensive. He stood on the sidewalk near the saloon's entrance and waited for me to park in front of his car.

I swung open the door and started to get out, glancing back up the street.

The front end of a muddy pickup truck bore down on me.

I jerked in my head and leg just as the truck plowed into the side of the Olds. It hammered the car with a heavy glancing blow, ripping off the door, tearing into the fender, and slamming the front end up onto the curb.

I was thrown to my left as the car was literally knocked out from under me. I grabbed the steering wheel, or I would've been tossed out into the street.

The truck roared away down Fifteenth Street, swerving slightly as if to regain its balance. It went the wrong way on the one-way viaduct leading out of downtown, barely avoiding a head-on with a green VW.

Drunken son of a bitch.

I fumbled the key into the ignition, fired up the Olds, slammed it into gear, and took off after him—right up onto the sidewalk. The steering wheel wouldn't budge, so I hit the brakes and shut off the engine. The last I saw of the truck was its tail end disappearing over the hump in the viaduct.

I climbed out, which was pretty easy, since the door was lying in the street.

Wes Hartman hurried toward me. A few people had come out of the bar and stood by the entrance, staring.

"Jesus Christ, are you all right?" Hartman gawked at me as if I were covered with blood.

I felt around, but I was dry and apparently unbroken.

"I think so, considering."

My car, though, was a mess. Everything from the door-post to the front bumper was caved in. Jagged metal gripped the tire like a claw. The end of the wraparound bumper stuck out as if it were signaling for a left turn. My poor baby. I dragged the door out of the street and leaned it against the car.

"Guy must've been drunk. Or crazy."

"Tell me." I was thinking that the truck looked a lot like the one Elliot the pool player was driving earlier today in Golden.

Hartman and I went into Brother's, and I called the police. Then the bartender poured me a Jack Daniel's on the rocks and on the house. Hartman sat at a table with me, shoved his aviators on top of his head, and sipped a club soda. The place was empty except for a few guys and gals at the bar. They kept sneaking glances at me, as if I were the famous actor who'd starred in *The Great Crash Outside*.

My hand trembled a little as I drank my bourbon. Adrenaline overdose. Or residual anger. Or maybe I was trying not to think about where I'd be right now if I hadn't glanced back and seen the truck.

"Are you sure you're all right?" Hartman asked.

"I'm okay."

"Well, *I'm* still shaking. If that guy had come along a minute earlier, he would've creamed *me*."

"You didn't happen to get his license number, did you?"

"No, I mean, it all happened so fast. First I saw you and I thought, Wow, what a coincidence, and then—"

"It wasn't a coincidence."

"Excuse me?"

"I followed you here."

"You what?" He grinned, waiting for the punch line.

"I wanted to talk to you alone, but you drove off before I could stop you. It's about the glass pipe I showed you in Kenneth Butler's office."

His face slowly lost all expression. "What about it?"

"You've seen it before, haven't you? Or one like it."

"What makes you say that?"

"Come on, Hartman, I'm not accusing you of anything. I'm just looking for information. Tell me what the pipe's for."

His eyes shifted to the side, as if he were thinking it over. He sipped his soda, then set down the glass. "It's for smoking ice."

"Ice?"

"A pure form of methamphetamine."

I'd read something about ice—a designer drug for the nineties, produced in a few Asian countries. It was already a big problem in Hawaii, more so, even, than crack.

"How do you know?" I asked.

He shrugged. "I've smoked it." Then he added earnestly, "Look, I'm no drug addict. I hardly even drink." He held up his glass to show me his soda. My glass was already empty. Hey, I'd been in an accident. "But I've tried this and that," Hartman went on to say. "Lots of things. In my business, sometimes you have to smoke or snort or drink like the client to get on his good side. It's just business."

"So Clare smoked ice."

"If she had a pipe like that, I'd say it's a good bet."

"Did you ever smoke it with her?"

"No, I told—"

"Or know where she bought it?"

Hartman gave me what passed for a hard look. "I *told* you, I'm not into that stuff. I've smoked ice once, period. And I knew very little about Clare Butler's personal life, let alone her drug habits."

I guess I believed him. "What *can* you tell me about Clare."

"Not much," he said. "I've only been a member of the family for eight months."

He'd met Nicole Butler last March at a tennis club. It had been love at first sight, and they'd wanted to get married right away. Her father objected. "He never liked me," Hartman said, "probably never will." However, Samuel Butler could see that Wes Hartman made his little girl happy, so he finally gave them his blessing. After the marriage, Butler offered Hartman a job with the company.

"I knew sales, so that's where I fit in," he said.

"What about Clare?"

Hartman shrugged. "I'd see her at family dinners, once a month or so. Maybe half a dozen times altogether."

"Where was this?"

"Sometimes at restaurants, sometimes at Sam's house." Hartman smiled. "He loves his kids, and he wants to preserve his big happy family."

I couldn't tell whether Hartman's smile was sincere or sardonic. With a salesman you can never be sure.

I asked him, "Do you know if Clare was having an affair?"

He pursed his lips and shook his head. "No. But it wouldn't surprise me."

"Why not?"

He shrugged. "She was young, and Samuel is old."

"Right. By the way, where were you when she was murdered?"

He shrugged again. "Home with my wife."

A uniformed cop walked in, and the bartender pointed at me.

"The one time you smoked ice," I said to Hartman as the cop walked over, "where was it?"

"Who was involved in the accident?"

"California," Hartman said.

I nodded and stood. "I was."

The cop filled out his report, writing down my vague description of the mud-spattered truck. As far as law enforcement went, it was mostly a meaningless ritual.

When we went outside, there was a tow truck waiting, leering over the Olds like a buzzard over a dead rabbit.

I rode in the truck to the garage on west Thirty-eighth Avenue where I'd had the Olds put back together just a few months ago. It was run by a guy named Harvey, a small, bald man with Popeye's forearms.

"Holy fucking shit," Harvey said when he saw the car.

"Don't worry, I wasn't hurt."

"What did you *do* to her?"

It was obvious where his sentiments lay. "How long will it take to fix?"

He folded his oversized arms and shook his head at the Olds. "Holy fucking shit," he said sadly.

Harvey wouldn't make any promises about cost or time. However, he did say I was in luck; his one loaner was available. Now normally I wouldn't call a twelve-year-old faded brown Toyota Corolla with a cracked windshield, torn upholstery, and dents in every fender luck. But at least I wouldn't have to put out cash for a rental.

"She uses oil," Harvey said. "Best to check it every few days."

I transferred a few things from the Olds's glove compartment, then rattled away in a cloud of blue smoke.

CHAPTER

8

I DROVE HOME AND CALLED Westfall's office to give him the names I'd found. No answer. My workday was done.

I probably should've been out looking for the flower vendor. But I was beat. I'd done more driving today than I had in months. Plus my nervous system was jumping with aftershocks—I'd come *that* close to being crushed by that goddamn truck.

I filled a glass with ice and Jack Daniel's and thought about the truck.

I'd had only the briefest view of the front end: mud-spattered grille partially hidden behind an oversized bumper. The bumper was black steel with twin vertical posts, like those on traffic-cop cars, for pushing stalled vehicles. There may have been a crossbar between the posts, too, but I was too busy getting out of the way to study it in detail.

Nor did I see the driver's face or even how many people were in the truck as it had crashed on by.

But there was no denying that the truck looked like Elliot's from Golden. Although that *had* to be a coincidence, because there was absolutely no reason for Elliot to want to kill me. At least none that I knew of.

A knock on the door. It was Vaz.

"Am I disturbing you, Jacob?"

MICHAEL ALLEGRETTO

"Not at all. Come in."

Vaz wore a heavy wool cardigan over his plaid flannel shirt. When you reach your sixties, spring still feels like winter. He had thick arms, a barrel chest, and broad shoulders, plus an oversized head to go with them. His trouser-draped legs, though, were spindly things, products of a childhood disease, ill treated by the village doctor.

"We haven't seen much of you since your return from Mexico."

"I know. I'm sorry. I've been meaning to stop by."

"Good. Because Sophia wants you to come down to dinner this evening. She is cooking a roast."

"Sounds great."

The Botvinnovs' apartment was filled with the warm, heavy smell of a simmering roast. It was also filled with furniture, Sophia's passion. She'd been raised in poverty in Soviet Georgia and now buried the memory with armchairs, ottomans, settees, and occasional tables.

"Hello, Jacob," Sophia called from the kitchen.

I followed Vaz through the maze, past a dining-room table so hemmed in by couches and credenzas that to eat there we'd have to stand up. We entered the relative openness of the kitchen, where the table was set for dinner.

Sophia gave me a brief but hefty hug, her huge bosom like sofa cushions against my abdomen. I kissed the top of her head.

"Smells wonderful in here," I said.

She nodded and brushed a strand of gray hair from her shiny, flushed face. "How have you been, Jacob? We've missed you."

"Just fine. Sorry I've been such a stranger."

"Mmm-hmm. Tell me," she said, attempting to sound

52

offhanded, pulling open the oven door, "are you seeing anyone now?"

I tried not to smile. Sophia never gave up.

"Seeing? What do you mean?"

"Jacob, now you know. Is there presently a young woman in your life?"

"Sophia," Vaz cautioned.

"Vassily, make yourself useful and open the wine," she snapped.

He gave me a weak smile and shrugged his shoulders. "Well, Jacob?"

There had been a woman before Mexico, but it ended almost before it got started. "No, not at present."

"Mmm-hmm," she said with meaning.

And sure enough, during dinner, after I'd told them about Puerto Vallarta and they'd described their warm-weather winter in Phoenix, Sophia said, "By the way, Jacob, I met a very nice young lady the other day in my church group."

Vaz groaned.

Sophia gave him a withering look, then turned a smile on me. "She's not much older than you and recently divorced. Her husband was a scoundrel. Anyway, she makes wonderful clothes, and I understand that she can cook, too."

"Well, I . . ."

"Perhaps some evening we will have you both here for dinner?"

"Well . . . perhaps."

"There," she said, looking at Vaz in triumph. He raised his brows, closed his eyes, made a face, and shook his head.

After the meal, Vaz and I helped his wife with the dishes. Then we set up the chessboard and poured brandy, while Sophia retired to the other room to "make some phone calls." I hoped one of them wasn't to the church lady.

"You are working on a case now?" Vaz asked, opening with pawn to queen four.

"Yes." I brought out my king's knight, intending to play the Grünfeld Defense, in which White establishes a strong pawn center and Black hammers away at it. I felt optimistic, confident, possibly because Vaz had removed his queen's rook from the board. Not that I could beat him with rook odds, but at least the game would last longer. "Possibly my last."

"Your last case?" His shaggy eyebrows jumped up like a pair of startled gerbils. "What do you mean?"

"I'm thinking about a career change."

"You're joking."

"No."

"But why? I thought you enjoyed what you did."

I shrugged. "Maybe it's time to move on to bigger and better things."

"Oh. Well, Jacob, change is often beneficial." He began developing his queen's side. "What are you going to do?"

"I haven't decided yet."

He frowned at me. I fianchettoed my king's bishop and castled.

"Is there something troubling you, Jacob? Something you'd like to talk about?"

"Not really."

"I see. Well, then, let us hear all about your *final* case."

I smiled at his sarcasm and told him about the murder of Clare Butler. He listened closely, nodding, castling, shoving his center pawns down my throat.

"It sounds as if you believe Samuel Butler is innocent."

"I'm leaning that way," I said. "Especially after having talked to Winks."

"Then who do you believe murdered his wife?"

"I don't know. Possibly her lover."

"If she had a lover."

"According to Butler, she did."

"Yes, according to him."

"Are you implying he's lying?"

"Jacob, I am only offering alternatives."

"Right, well, there were no signs of a break-in or struggle, so Clare knew her killer."

"A friend."

"According to Kenneth Butler, she had no friends."

"A relative, then."

"There's a thought," I said. "Let's see, there are Samuel's three children—Kenneth, Karen, and Nicole—plus Wes Hartman and Kenneth's wife, Doreen."

"You include the women?" He invaded my camp with his knight. His queen and dark-squared bishop weren't far behind.

"Why not, while we're speculating."

"But would a woman be capable of bashing in someone's head with a wrench?"

"If you mean physically, no problem."

"And psychologically?"

"Whoever killed Clare was either crazed or filled with hate," I said. "Sex wouldn't matter in the least."

"I see. Check."

"Shit."

It wasn't long before I resigned. We set up the pieces for another game. I must've winced, moving my arm, because Vaz asked me, "Are you in pain?"

"Just a little sore." I told him about my accident that afternoon.

He was horrified. "My God, Jacob, you could have been killed."

"Occupational hazard."

"That is nothing to joke about." Then he studied me from beneath heavy brows. "Is this why you want to quit your profession? The danger?"

"No."

"What of this accident? Did it have anything to do with your case?"

"It was completely unrelated." I still could think of no reason for Elliot to follow me from Golden and try to run me down. Unless . . . What if Butler had had an ulterior motive for driving to Golden on the day of the murder? Something involving Elliot. . . .

"Jacob?"

"What?"

"It is your move."

CHAPTER

9

THE NEXT MORNING, I woke up with a stiff back and a sore right arm, remnants from the accident. I loosened up with some stretching exercises and half an hour of sit-ups and push-ups. After a hot shower and a shave, I warmed four bagel halves in the toaster oven, then loaded them with cream cheese, chopped onion, sliced tomato, and smoked salmon.

I carried my second cup of coffee onto the balcony.

It was a bright, crisp morning, and the sun felt warm on my face. Two stories below me, in the backyard, old George was manually aerating the lawn. Each time he pushed the long-handled tool into the ground, up would pop two finger-sized plugs of dirt. Mrs. Finch stood nearby, giving him step-by-step instructions, fists on hips, head bobbing like a bird's.

I finished my coffee and phoned Oliver Westfall. He wasn't in his office yet, but his secretary took the information: names and numbers for two of his three witnesses—Randy Stilwell and Russ "Winks" Armbruster.

I spent the next hour on the phone trying to find out who sold curb-side flowers on South Colorado Boulevard. When I finally found the company—All-City Vendors—they'd cheerfully checked their files for the employee's name who'd worked the Denny's parking lot on the fateful afternoon of March sixteenth. Of course, I'd had to lie (by omission). I'd said I was (private) Detective Lomax working (for the accused) on a murder case. They gave me the guy's address, too.

The apartment house was just off Thirteenth Street in Capitol Hill.

It's a densely populated area, about equally black and white, all equally poor. It has one of the higher crime rates in the city—burglaries, rapes, and drugs. The decent people still outnumbered the scum, though, so most of the buildings were well-tended, with tiny little yards sloping down to the street.

A lot of the buildings had names as well as numbers. The one I wanted was called Mar-Vista. An inspiration, considering the nearest ocean was two hours away by jet.

I stood in the stale-smelling vestibule and read the pencilled-in paper tags that were Scotch-taped to the mail boxes. Number 211 listed "Colodny, C. & Marling, P." I pushed the buzzer a few times, then held it down for a full minute. If no one was home, maybe I'd pop the locks and go up there anyway, just to see if I still had it in me. But then a man answered, his voice furry with sleep and tinny from the intercom.

"Who is it?"

"Are you Charles Colodny?"

"Yeah, so?"

I told him who I was and asked if he'd answer a few questions. "May I come up?"

"Questions about what?"

"You may have valuable information concerning a murder."

"Murder?" Some of the sleep had gone out of his voice. Not much, though—he still sounded groggy. "Who got murdered?"

"A woman named Clare Butler."

"Clare who?"

"May I come up, please."

A pause, and then he buzzed me in.

I went up two half-flights of stairs and down a hallway. The carpeting was worn and stained and musty, and the walls needed paint. The door to 211 was already open when I got there.

The guy standing in the doorway was around twenty, average height, and skinny. His T-shirt was baggy and so were his jeans, the belt-ends flopping unhooked. He was barefoot. His toes were gnarly. But then, whose weren't?

"Clare who?" he asked me again. His tone of voice was anxious, but his eyes were droopy, as if he were having trouble keeping them open.

"Butler. Shall we go inside?"

"Oh. Sure."

The living room and the kitchen were both small, separated by a countertop. The furniture was secondhand, but everything was as neat as if the cleaning lady had just left. Throw pillows were geometrically arranged on the couch, the glass ashtrays were wiped clean, and a few issues of *Playboy* and *Cosmopolitan* were squarely stacked on the coffee table. There wasn't one dirty dish in the kitchen sink.

"I've never heard of Clare Butler," he said. His face stretched in a yawn; then he squinted and blinked his eyes a few times. He moved nervously from one foot to the other. Maybe they were cold. "Are you sure it's not Patti you want to talk to?" He glanced nervously behind him. "She's at work now."

"No, Charles, it's you. You—"

"Chuck."

"Chuck. You sell flowers for All-City Vendors, right? In the Denny's parking lot on South Colorado Boulevard?"

"Sure." He kept glancing over his shoulder.

"On Saturday, March sixteenth, do you remember a—"

"Would, ah, would you excuse me a minute?"

Before I could respond, he left the room, picking up something from the kitchen counter on his way out. He went down a short hall to the bedroom and closed the door behind him.

I'd gotten only a glimpse of what he'd lifted from the counter, but I'd recognized it immediately. It looked like the one I had in my pocket—a small glass pipe. See? Coincidences *do* happen.

While I waited for Chuck, I copied the number on his phone. Then I sat on the couch and flipped through *Playboy*. Miss April was a receptionist who would prefer a career in international diplomacy. Her hobbies included volleyball, jet skiing, rock music, painting her nails, and working with the elderly. She also enjoyed lounging naked around the house while some stranger snapped her picture.

I stood when I heard the bedroom door open.

Chuck had put on white socks, running shoes, and a polo shirt. The tail was tucked in, and his belt was buckled. His smile was easy and confident. He looked wide awake now, full of energy.

"Sorry," he said. "I just had to wake up."

I took a shot. "Ice is nice."

He gave me a knowing grin and began straightening the magazines. Then he stopped, frowning.

"Wait a minute, are you a goddamn narc?"

"Relax," I said. "I've got one just like yours." I showed him Clare Butler's pipe. He eyed it suspiciously. I put it away and got out the Butlers' photo. "Do you recognize this man?"

Chuck blinked at me a couple of times, maybe still thinking about the pipe. Then he studied the photo.

"Nice-looking babe," he said.

"What about the man? You ever seen him before?"

He shook his head, still looking at the photo. "Nope."

"He says he bought flowers from you on Saturday, March sixteenth, around three-thirty in the afternoon."

Chuck shrugged. "A lot of people buy flowers."

"He says he gave you a hundred-dollar bill and told you to keep the change."

His face opened up in a grin. "Hey, hell yes, I remember."

Before I could say, "Good," Chuck said, "So this is the guy, huh? I didn't pay much attention to his face. I was looking at that bill."

Swell. I told him that Butler's attorney would be calling him today or tomorrow to answer some more questions.

"Sure, whatever," Chuck said, all traces of nervousness gone. He was still in motion, but it seemed more purposeful than before. He nudged the coffee table an inch closer to the couch, then began repositioning the throw pillows.

"What can you tell me about ice?"

He faced me holding a pillow to his chest with both hands.

"A friend wants me to try it," I said, "but I'm kind of afraid."

He gave me a half grin. "There's nothing to be afraid of. Except, you know, narcs." His brow furrowed. "And you're not one, right?"

"That's correct. Tell me about ice. Is it addictive?"

"Hey, no way. I smoke it four or five times a week, and I can quit whenever I want." His face brightened. "You want to try it?"

"Well . . ."

"Wait a minute."

He left the room and returned with his glass pipe and a disposable lighter. In the ball end of the pipe was a small clump of translucent crystals, like sea salt. Chuck covered the tiny hole at the top of the ball with his thumb, clicked the lighter, and touched the flame to the glass. Almost at once the crystals melted and bubbled, then vaporized. Wisps of odorless white smoke swirled inside the ball, like the clouds of heaven.

Chuck held out the pipe to me.

"You go ahead," I said.

He sucked in the smoke, inhaling deeply. Then he exhaled and smiled.

"I mean, it makes your mind so *clear*," he said. "It doesn't mess you up like grass. And it's a helluva lot better than crack." He handed me the pipe.

"How so?" I set the pipe aside. Chuck didn't seem to notice.

"This costs about the same, maybe a little more. But a hit of crack would last me, what, fifteen, twenty minutes? Hell, this'll keep me going till midnight, maybe later. And you know the best part."

"No."

"I feel like working. I mean, I wish I could go to work right now, swinging those bouquets, rapping to the folks in their cars. I love it, I'm outside, I got the sunshine, my music pumping through my headset, and they *pay* me, it's great. Now you take my old lady Patti. She's got this part-time job downtown, a filing clerk. She smokes a little ice, and I mean, she is a filing fool. They've never *seen* anybody file like that. They gave her a raise. Shit, pretty soon they'll probably put her on full-time. What other drug can make that statement." He laughed at his own joke. "Of course, Patti also likes it because she's trying to lose some weight, and it's great for that, too, because you've got all this energy, but you're not really hungry, you know what I mean?"

"Where can I buy some?"

He frowned. "I don't know, man, it's pretty hard to find. I get it from a dude who gets it from a dude who has it mailed to him from Honolulu. But my dude's pretty paranoid about dealing to strangers." Chuck grinned. "Actually, he's pretty paranoid most of the time. For a while he thought the narcs had bugged his brain so they could listen to his thoughts. Weird, huh? Ice can do that. But he's better now."

As Chuck talked, he'd been edging toward the kitchen. Now he picked up a dish towel and began wiping the already sterile countertop.

I thanked him for his help and left him to his housework.

I walked to the car, thinking about the witnesses for Samuel Butler: a bartender who couldn't say when Butler left the bar, a guy who shoots at UFOs, and a kid addicted to ice.

The defense rests.

CHAPTER

10

I STOPPED AT A CONVENIENCE STORE on Thirteenth Avenue. Years ago I'd been called to a robbery in progress at this very location. Maybe that's why the three kids standing with their heads together near the entrance looked as if they were planning an armed robbery. But no, they were just conducting business. Money and small envelopes changed hands, and they went their separate ways.

I got change from the Iranian guy behind the counter, then went back outside and called Oliver Westfall from the pay phone. I gave him Chuck Colodny's name and numbers.

"That's all three witnesses, then," he said. "Good job. I'll personally phone each of them today and have them come in tomorrow for their depositions."

"Don't expect too much," I said. I explained that Stilwell the bartender barely remembered Butler and that Colodny hadn't even recognized his photo.

"What about Winks?" Westfall said. "He was with Mr. Butler for a few hours. Surely *he* can testify to his behavior."

"He can. But the problem might be Winks's behavior." I explained about the alien landings.

Westfall groaned quietly.

I offered, "There's still Clare Butler's lover."

"If such a person exists. We have only Mr. Butler's vague impressions."

"Does that mean you want me to give up the search?"

"What have you found so far?"

"Nothing."

Westfall was silent for a moment. "No, keep looking. Let me know when you find anything."

After we'd hung up, I phoned Kenneth Butler's sister Karen. I got an answering machine at her home. When I punched in her work number, a woman answered with "Second Time Around."

"Is this Karen?"

"This is Teri. Karen comes in at two."

I checked my watch. Eleven-thirty.

"Can I help you with something?" she asked.

"I just need to talk to her."

"Well, if it's urgent, you can find her at The Gym."

"Which gym is that?"

"*The* Gym. It's on East Hampden."

I got there before noon. The huge front windows of The Gym were all reflective glass so you could see how far out of shape you were *before*. I sucked in my gut and went inside.

There was a glass-fronted counter displaying bottles and jars of pills, powders, and capsules, all guaranteed to help you reach superhumanhood. The girl behind the counter figured she was already there. Her hot-pink spandex outfit showed off muscular arms, broad shoulders, and small, hard breasts. She gave me a healthy smile. But it began to fade when I said I wasn't a member. And it vanished forever when I declined to join. She did let me pass, however, after I told her I had an urgent message for Karen Butler.

"Check the bicycles," she said, consulting a clipboard.

I walked around the counter and down a short hallway,

then entered an enormous, brightly lit room filled with chrome-plated equipment and sweaty people, who ranged in age from mid-twenties to middle-age. Most of them appeared to be in pretty good shape already and were probably here on their lunch hour to socialize and check out each other's glutes. Over in one corner were the serious body builders, clanking free weights and popping steroids.

I spotted the stationary bicycles across the room. There were ten in a row, all occupied, each connected to its own computerized display. I asked for Karen Butler and was directed to the machine at the far end.

She was sitting on the bike, not pedaling, leaning forward and punching buttons beneath the monitor. A squat human mutant stood beside her.

"Come on," the mutant said, "you've got to extend yourself."

He reached toward the buttons. Karen pushed his hand away.

"Randy, why don't you go play with your weights," she said, annoyed.

"I'd rather help you."

"I don't need your help."

"Karen Butler?"

She turned and looked up at me. Except for the black hair, there was little resemblance between her and the male Butlers. Her cheekbones were high and delicate, and her nose was thin, aristocratic. Her face was very white, as if she carefully avoided the sun, and her pale hazel eyes seemed translucent. She wore shiny blue spandex that covered her the way a coat of paint would cover the statue of a nude.

"Yes?" she said, frowning at my street clothes.

"I'm Jacob Lomax, and I'm working for your father's attorney. Would you mind if I asked you a few questions?"

"Now? I'm right in the middle of—"

"She's in the middle of her workout," Randy the Mutant said.

He wore red bikini briefs and nothing else. Mid-twenties, I'd say, half a foot shorter than I was, no more than five seven. But he must've weighed 220, all of it mutated humps of lamp-tanned muscle. His thigh muscles were so big it made him bowlegged. Veins crawled like worms over his pumped-up biceps and forearms. His wrists and hands looked ridiculously small. Hey, nobody's perfect.

"We can talk while you pedal," I said to Karen.

"Did you hear what I said?" Randy wanted to know.

"That is, if it's all right with you."

"I guess so."

"Hey, I'm talking to you." Randy waddled around the rear of the stationary bike and planted his bulk between me and Karen. He smelled faintly sour. You see? This is what I hate about this job.

"Hey, give us a break," I said.

"I could break something on you, buddy."

"Like what, my olfactory lobes?"

His eyes went to slits.

Karen said, "Randy, why don't you parade your macho shit in front of the other steroid freaks and let us talk in privacy."

Randy hesitated, then poked me in the chest with two fingers. It hurt. "I'll talk to *you* later," he said. Then he waddled away, showing us lats the size of cafeteria trays.

I turned to Karen. "Sorry about the interruption."

"Don't be silly, you did me a favor. The guy's a jerk."

Karen leaned forward and fiddled with some buttons. A colored computer image came on the screen. A black road stretched out before her through a green-and-brown landscape. There was a bicyclist on either side, one in blue, one in red. The two cyclists began to pull ahead. Karen pedaled, and the riders fell back.

"How did you know to find me here?"

"Teri told me."

"You were at the shop?"

"I phoned. What is it, anyway, Second Time Around?"

"We sell vintage clothing."

"You're partners?"

"I own the business." She kept her eyes on the screen and said, "You said you're working for Oliver Westfall. Which means you're working for my father."

"Yes. They hired me to find the people your father spoke to the day Clare was killed."

"Can they prove he's innocent?"

"Well, no, but—"

"Then what good are they?" she asked, a flash of heat in her voice, like lightning. As quickly, it was gone. Her eyes had never left the screen. "I'm sorry. I didn't mean to sound bitter."

"I understand."

"But all this is so . . . trying. On everyone."

Karen was pedaling faster now, trying to stay ahead of the two men. The red-shirted guy kept nudging up on her left. She held her lead, though, her long, shapely legs pumping in a steady rhythm. The road before her swung left and then right. There were mountains dead ahead.

"There's one more person I need to find," I said. "And I was hoping you could help me."

"Who is it?"

"Clare's lover."

Karen shot me a glance, breaking her rhythm. The two cyclists moved ahead of her. She faced the screen again and pedaled hard to catch up. Her fists were clenched on the handlebars, her arm muscles were rigid, and her face was set in fierce determination. Now she resembled her father and brother.

She spoke at last, a bit breathless, having overtaken the

two riders. "Which of Clare's lovers are you looking for? The woman was a slut."

"Oh? Then her latest one. Your father believes she was involved with someone at the time of her death."

"I know. That's why he k—"

Like her brother, she had trouble saying it, but she believed it just the same—that her father had murdered Clare.

Then she asked, "What good would it do if you found her lover?"

"Hard to say."

"Well, I don't know who it was."

"Anything you can tell me about Clare would help. Your father, that is."

Karen continued to pump the bike, her gaze focused on the screen as if she were willing herself into that simple, safe, two-dimensional world. Then she stopped. She sat there, breathing hard, staring straight ahead. The two bicyclists passed her by and pedaled off into the distance. She switched off the monitor.

"Let me take a quick shower and we'll talk."

She climbed off the bike. She was taller than I'd thought, almost as tall as her brother. I told her I'd wait outside. She nodded and walked away. A lovely walk. I went through the lobby to the parking lot.

Oh, swell.

Randy the Mutant was waiting for me.

CHAPTER

11

RANDY HAD DRESSED FOR THE OCCASION: blue sweatpants, white high-tops, and a triple-extra-large T-shirt. The shirt stretched across his multilevel chest, distorting the stylized weight lifter on the front. The lifter looked a bit like Randy. He probably wasn't much smarter, either, because he was trying to clean and jerk a set of barbells the size of locomotive wheels.

"You and me got unfinished business," he said.

" 'You and I *have* . . .' "

"Huh?"

"Look, Randy, there's no reason for this. It's what they call gratuitous violence."

"You want violence, pal, I'll show you violence."

"That's not what I—"

He scooted toward me like a giant crab—chin down, arms up, elbows out. I backpedaled, smack into the side of a Chevy van. Randy grabbed two fistfuls of my jacket and shirt, lifted me clear off my feet, and began slamming me against the van. I could've punched him, but there was nothing to hit but the top of his thick head and shoulders the size of prize pigs. Meanwhile, he was knocking the air out of my lungs and bruising my kidneys. Who needs this?

In between body slams I unholstered the .38. I brought it up inside Randy's overdeveloped arms and pressed its snub nose to his snub nose, bending his up a bit more than nature had intended.

He froze, holding me at arm's length, my back against the van and my toes barely touching the ground. His eyes were crossed, looking down at the gun.

"Here's the iron I pump, Randy."

He couldn't move his eyes from the gun. In fact, he was afraid to move anything, because I was still pinned to the van, dancing on my toes.

"Down, boy," I said.

Slowly, he put me down, let go of my jacket, and backed away.

"Ta ta," I told him, and waved good-bye with the .38. He turned and walked toward the entrance, a man of fewer words than I, giving me one last look over his deltoid—red-faced hatred. Another satisfied customer.

I put away the gun, straightened my lapels, and waited for Karen. Ten minutes later, she came out wearing swirl-colored tights and a baggy yellow sweater that reached nearly to mid-thigh. A small gym bag was slung over her shoulder.

"Sorry to make you wait," she said.

"No problem. Randy kept me company."

She frowned. "Randy? What did—"

"Say, I usually eat lunch about now. Are you hungry?"

Her frown lasted a moment longer before she said, "Famished. There's a deli just up the street. I'll drive."

I squeezed into her bright white Mazda Miata, and we took off with a well-modulated roar.

The deli was tucked in the corner of a small shopping complex on the north side of Hampden. To the left, as we walked in, was a display counter of kosher fish and meats and a rack of freshly bagged bagels. To the right was the restaurant area—tables and booths with red vinyl seats. It was nearly full, buzzing with conversations, but we managed to get a booth against the wall.

My wife Katherine had liked this place. We'd come here frequently, usually for Sunday breakfast. It struck me that this was the first time I'd been back since she'd died—nearly five years ago. Had I consciously avoided coming here? I wondered what else I'd been avoiding.

The waitress hobbled over on sore feet and took our orders: corned beef on light rye and a Bud for me, matzo ball soup for Karen.

"I thought you said you were famished."

"It doesn't take much to fill me up." She gave me a weak smile, then looked down at the table and fiddled with her silverware. "Do you . . . think he killed her?" She'd spoken quietly so her voice wouldn't carry beyond our booth.

"No."

She looked up, surprised. "I mean, really."

"Really."

"Why?" she asked me flatly. "All the evidence says he did. And I *know* he's capable of something like that."

"How do you mean?"

"You answer first. Why don't you think my father killed Clare?"

"For one thing, the way he behaved in Golden that day, not like a man with murder on his mind. And for another, something he said to me yesterday at the jail: 'She was mine, and he took her from me.' He talked about Clare's killer as if the man were a thief instead of a murderer."

"I'm not sure I see the significance."

"Maybe there is none. But if your father had killed Clare and were trying to convince me otherwise, I think he would've behaved differently. More horrified by her death. Instead, he spoke as if he'd been robbed of a possession."

"Possession," Karen said bitterly. "That fits. He sees people as things. He thinks he can own them—his employees, his children . . ."

The waitress showed up with our food. We ate for a time in silence. I spread more red horseradish on my corned beef and asked, "What did you mean when you said your father was capable of killing Clare?"

She sipped her soup and gave me a small shrug. "His temper. He'd get mad, and he'd hit. He's hit us all—me, my brother, even my mother. Clare, too, of course."

"You left out your sister."

"Nicole?" She smiled without mirth. "Oh, no, not her. She's always been Daddy's little girl. Kenneth was seven and I was six when she was born. My father spoiled her rotten, gave her anything she wanted." She set down her spoon, her eyes sad. "Of course, he gave me and Kenneth plenty, too. Material things. Everything except . . ."

"What?"

"Love." She shook her head. "He was never affectionate with me. And certainly not with Kenneth. And if he ever showed my mother any tenderness, it must've been in their bedroom with the door closed, because I never saw it." She blew air through her aristocratic nose. "I guess he was saving it for baby Nicole. And maybe later for Clare."

So much for the big happy family.

"Kenneth told me that you knew Clare first."

She sighed and nudged the bowl away from her. It was still half-filled with broth, and there were only a few small craters in the matzo ball.

"Yes," she said.

"How did you meet her?"

"Does it really matter?"

"I don't know, does it?"

She turned her head and stared across the room at the entrance, as if she wanted to leave.

Finally, she said, "I met Clare two years ago in Aspen."

Karen explained how she'd taken an extended weekend, skiing with some friends. But on her first run she'd twisted her knee. She'd limped around the lodge on crutches for the entire three days. Clare was there with a male companion from Kansas City. Since she'd never skied in her life, she was effectively stranded in the lodge, too. She and Karen gravitated toward each other, and by the end of the three days they were friends.

Six months later, Clare had walked into Karen's shop in need of money, a job, and a place to live.

"She'd been forced to leave her home in Kansas City," Karen said. "She had no one to turn to. I was the closest thing she had to a friend."

"What do you mean she was 'forced to leave'?"

"I never learned all the details. Only that it was something very unpleasant for her and that it had to do with her male friend."

"The man she'd been with in Aspen?"

"Yes."

"I don't suppose you remember his name."

"As a matter of fact, I do. His last name, anyway. Rockefeller. Who could forget that?"

"Is he the one who forced her to leave Kansas City?"

"I don't know," Karen said. "Anyway, she was obviously down on her luck, so I gave her a part-time job. It wasn't as if Teri and I needed the help. We just wanted to help Clare. She knew how to . . . get things from people. I let her stay at my house until she found an apartment." Karen twisted her mouth in a bitter grin. "A month later, she found my father instead."

The waitress took away our plates.

74

I said, "Kenneth told me that you introduced Clare to your father."

She gave me a sour look. "Kenneth likes to believe it was my fault they got together. Yes, I introduced them. My father came into the shop about a month after I'd hired Clare." Karen snorted. "She was on him like a bee on honey. It wasn't until that moment that I realized what she really wanted, what she'd wanted from the start—a sugar daddy to take care of her. And she didn't care who—" Karen looked quickly away, but not before I'd seen the pain in her eyes. "She didn't care who she used in the process," she said.

Now she turned to me with such a look of hatred that I was briefly startled.

"I'm glad she's dead," Karen said in a low, mean voice. "I'm sorry for my father, but I'm glad that fucking bitch is in her grave." She smiled evilly. "Does that surprise you?"

"A bit." Actually, I was more surprised that she'd admitted it. It wasn't too hard to picture her standing over Clare with a wrench in her hand.

"I'll tell you something else," Karen said. "Kenneth and Nicole are glad she's dead, too."

"Did they tell you that?"

"They don't have to. I know how much they love money, my father's money. Eventually, we'll inherit it. But he was throwing it away on Clare as if there were no tomorrow—jewelry, clothes, trips abroad. Everything first-class. Nothing too good or expensive for precious little Clare." She blew air through her nose, then looked at her watch. "I have to get to work."

"Wait. You still haven't told me about Clare's lover. Or lovers."

"I don't know anything about them."

"You know she had lovers. Who were they?"

"I . . . don't know."

"You can't give me one name?" Even I knew one, because Butler had told me—Christopher Pruitt.

"No."

I'm sure she was lying, but I couldn't exactly twist her arm. She slid out of the booth, then waited impatiently while I paid the bill.

We roared off in her Miata almost before I got the passenger door closed. I fumbled with my seat belt as she swerved in and out of traffic and finally slid to a stop in the parking lot of The Gym.

"What was Clare's maiden name?"

"Dickerson. Look, I have to go."

"When did—"

"Look, I'm serious."

I unfolded myself out of the car and shut the door.

"I'd like to talk to you some more about—"

But she roared off, squealing the tires.

The sound reminded me of what Samuel Butler's neighbor had told me yesterday. He'd heard the squeal of tires in the driveway about the time Clare had been murdered.

Of course, a lot of people squeal their tires.

On the other hand, only one of them had told me she was glad Clare Butler was in her grave.

CHAPTER

12

I DROVE TO MY OFFICE.

It's on Broadway, not far from downtown. On the ground floor are a liquor store, a pawnshop, a greasy-spoon café, and a Christian Science Reading Room (formerly the Zodiac Bookstore, formerly the Christian Science Reading Room—the battle of good and evil goes on). On the second floor are me, a vacancy, a dentist who I wouldn't let polish my shoes, much less my teeth, and Acme, Inc.

I've never seen Mr. Acme, nor do I know what business he's in. But he's always on the phone. He was on it now as I passed by his door.

". . . arrived unassembled, Murray, in goddamn pieces. A thousand boxes of loose parts. How do I sell them, Murray, as puzzles, for God's sake? Never mind, just do me a favor. Call my wife. Tell her I'm having a heart attack because Murray now sends me puzzles. . . ."

I unlocked my door and went in, picking the mail off the floor. I'd had the post office resume delivery here only a few days ago, and already the junk was flowing. I dumped it all in the wastebasket.

I tossed my jacket on the leather couch, sat in the swivel chair behind the desk, and began flipping through the Rolodex. When I found the name I was looking for, I dialed long distance.

"*Kansas City Star*," the woman said.

I asked for the sports desk and then for Ed Nylund.

Ed had been a reporter for the *Denver Post* when I'd been in uniform. Occasionally, and always unofficially, we'd let news guys ride in the patrol car during our shift.

One night, with Ed in the backseat, my partner and I caught a squeal—robbery in progress at a convenience store on Thirteenth Avenue. As we pulled into the parking lot, two suspects were making their getaway. They rammed our patrol car, fired shots through our windshield, then sped away. We pursued, with glass in our laps and the wind in our hair, screaming through intersections, screeching around corners, speeding down alleys. A few blocks later, they ran a red light and got smacked by a taxi. Their car jumped the curb, took out thirty feet of picket fence, and crashed into the side of a house. The suspects rolled out, one on each side, shooting, putting a few more holes in the patrol car. We shot back and put holes in them.

After that it was a circus. The street was blocked with gawkers, backup units, tow trucks, and ambulances. A network affiliate was setting up bright lights and a camera when my partner asked me, "Where's Ed?"

I found him curled in a fetal position in the backseat of the patrol car, sprinkled with glass shards but otherwise unscathed. However, soon after that, he'd turned to sports. Sometime later, he and his family had moved to Kansas City.

"Ed Nylund," he said, coming on the line.

"Ed, Jake Lomax."

"Hey, Jake, how've you been?"

We bantered a bit before I said, "This is a long shot, but I figured if anyone could help me, it's you."

"Let's hear it."

"I'm on a case involving a woman named Clare Butler. She used to be Clare Dickerson from Kansas City, and she hung out with a guy named Rockefeller."

"John D. or Nelson A.?"

"Neither, I'm sure, but I don't know his first name. About a year and a half ago, Clare left him and K.C. under distressing circumstances. I don't know the details, but I figured if it'd been newsworthy—"

"I can check. Was this Kansas City, Missouri, or Kansas?"

"What's the difference?"

"Hey, pal, those are fighting words."

"Just kidding. I don't know which state."

"Okay. I'll call you back and let you know what I find."

"Today?"

"Hey, I've got real work to do."

"Yeah, but I saved your life."

He chuckled at our old joke. "So *you're* the one who told those bastards to shoot high so they wouldn't hit the scared-shitless reporter in the backseat."

"That was me."

"I'll see what I can do."

I bought the *News* and the *Post* and hung around the office for the rest of the afternoon studying the want ads. Plenty of jobs available. Telephone salesperson. Restaurant-manager trainee. Security guard. Sure, that's it, I'll put on a uniform and stand around a bank all day nodding hello to the customers.

I read the sports pages and worked the crossword puzzles.

Ed Nylund didn't call back.

I walked downstairs and outside. The rush-hour flow on Broadway thickened the air with an eye-watering, lung-searing fume. Above, the sky was overcast. If I could smell, it might have smelled like rain. Or snow—it was chilly enough.

I pushed into the greasy spoon, or as it was officially called on the window's painted sign: Café. There were some street people huddled in a booth nursing their coffee and a couple of uniformed cops at the counter doing the same. I took a stool and ordered the day's special— green beans, real mashed potatoes, and chicken-fried steak served with an extra-sharp knife. It wasn't bad. And the beers were cold.

Later, in my office, I looked up Wes Hartman's number. He'd been firm about me phoning before I came to his house. I dialed. It was busy. Well, I tried.

Wes and Nicole lived within a mile or so of Samuel Butler's house, in a pricey condo near University and Yale. It was a three-story brownish yellow concrete building with an irregular roofline, jutting buttresses, narrow windows, and a surrounding concrete wall. It looked like a scale model for a prison of the future. Maybe it was.

According to the glass-encased directory, there were two residences per floor. The Hartmans lived in "B," second level. I lifted the receiver and smiled up at the security camera.

"Yes?" A young woman's voice, wary.

"Nicole Hartman?"

"Yes?"

I told her who I was and for whom I was working. "If you're not busy, I'd like to ask you and Wes some questions."

"About Daddy?"

"About Clare."

"Well . . . Wes isn't home yet."

"I'll wait. Out here." Sigh. "In my car." Poor Jake.

She hesitated, then told me to come up.

Nicole Butler Hartman was in her early twenties, with short black hair and large dark eyes. She somewhat resembled her father and brother; her black eyebrows were knit in the infamous Butler scowl. It looked less threatening on her, though, almost cute. A little girl pouting. She wore black running shoes, black tights, and a billowy man's shirt, smudged with paint. The sleeves were rolled up to her elbows, forming huge cuffs and revealing thin, sinewy forearms. The pictures I'd seen of her at Butler's house showed her to be over-weight. No more.

"I was working," she said, explaining her clothes.

She led me into the living room.

It was furnished somewhat like the one in her father's house—white leather couch and chairs. But here they seemed uninviting. Sterile and cold.

The walls were bone white. The one behind the couch was hung with a four-foot-square oil painting in a chrome frame. The canvas depicted a nightmare landscape in purple and black. In the background, beneath a sickly green-ish sky, tiny blackened figures reached upward. It was difficult to tell whether they were humans or blasted trees.

"What did you want to know about Clare?" Nicole asked dully. She stood in the center of the room, left arm at her side, right arm across her body, hand holding elbow.

"I'm trying to find out who—"

"Daddy didn't kill her." She glanced nervously over her shoulder, as if there were someone waiting in another room.

"No, I don't think he did, either."

"I *know* he didn't. He . . . wouldn't." There was a wild, frightened look in her eyes. Wes had told me that Butler's arrest had devastated Nicole. I believed him.

"Your father thinks Clare was having an affair," I said.

81

Nicole nodded tightly, shooting looks over her shoulder. Her fingers drummed a beat on her elbow.

"Was she?"

"If Daddy says so, then she was."

"Do—"

"Can we talk in my studio? I was in the middle of something."

Without waiting for a reply, Nicole walked out. Her actions reminded me of Chuck Colodny, the flower vendor. I followed her down a hallway past a few closed doors to a converted bedroom at the end.

In the center of the room, highlighted by overhead track lighting, stood a heavy wooden easel, its uprights nearly touching the ceiling. A flat-topped cabinet squatted beside it holding a smeared palette, tubes of paint, and jars of brushes. The hardwood floor was splotched with paint. There were a dozen or so large canvases leaning in stacks against the wall. The ones I could see looked a lot like the one in the living room. So did the painting in progress on the easel—dark, swirling colors, tiny black semihuman shapes. More like things than people.

Nicole picked up her easel and a brush and began daubing the sky with a lovely shade of black.

I asked, "Who do you think Clare was seeing behind your father's back?"

"I have no idea."

"Did she have *any* friends that you know about?"

"No." Then she hesitated, her brush hovering above the canvas. "Well, there was a woman . . ."

"Yes?"

"I only saw her once. I'd gone to my father's house to get some mon—to talk to him about something. He wasn't there, but when I walked in, I found this woman in the living room, flipping through a magazine. She said she was waiting for Clare. And then Clare came in and told me Daddy had gone to the liquor store and that when he got back I should tell him she'd gone shopping. Then they left."

"What was the woman's name?"

"Madeline something." She resumed blackening the sky with nervous little strokes.

"Madeline what?"

"Hmm." Then she smiled for the first time since I'd arrived. She stopped painting and held her brush up to me as if she were showing me a new toy. "Tate," she said. "Madeline Tate."

"Where can I find her?"

She resumed painting. "How should I know?"

"Is there anyone else you can think of? Any other friends?"

"No."

"Any enemies."

Her brush stopped, an inch from the canvas. She stared at it wickedly, as if it were a bothersome insect she was about to squash. "I can think of a few," she said, and jabbed the painting.

"Who?"

"Everyone in my family."

"Do you mean you and—"

"I mean *all of us!*" Her voice had risen to a screech. Now she clamped her jaws and squeezed her eyes closed, holding it in. Her hand was a small, hard fist around her brush. I figured a wrench could fit in there quite easily. She blinked her eyes and spoke with measured fury. "We . . . All . . . Hated . . . Her."

"So I've heard. Because she was spending your inheritance."

She turned to me, her face twisted in rigid folds. "It wasn't the money we cared about. It was *Daddy*. She was taking him from us."

Before I could ask her to elaborate, we both heard the front door open.

Nicole's expression turned as dark as her painting. She slammed down her palette and brush and strode from the studio. I followed as far as the entryway to the front room.

Wes Hartman was taking off his jacket.

"Where have you been?" Nicole's voice cracked like a whip.

Wes didn't even flinch. "Out," he said, and tossed his jacket on the nearest leather chair.

"You've been drinking. I can smell it on your breath."

"So what."

"Where were you."

"What diff— Hey."

He saw me standing in the doorway. I entered the room.

"Hi, Wes, we've been waiting for you."

"What the hell are you doing here?"

Nicole got in his face. "I want to know where you were."

Wes stepped around her. "I thought I told you to call before you ever came over here."

"I tried but—"

"Answer me," Nicole snapped, as if I weren't in the room.

"I want you out of here now," Wes told me, ignoring his wife.

"I was just leaving," I said.

Wes slammed the door behind me. I stood for a moment in the hallway, not exactly pressing my ear to the door but not leaning away, either.

"What was he doing here?" I heard Wes ask, his voice muffled by the door.

"Goddammit, I want to know where—"

"First you tell me why he was here?"

"Why do you think? He was asking about Clare."

"What exactly did you— Wait."

I heard him move toward the door, so I hustled around the corner and ducked down the stairs before he got it open.

Eavesdropping makes me feel so cheap.

CHAPTER

13

IT SNOWED THAT NIGHT.

Not much, just enough to wet the streets and drape the neighborhood's greening lawns in a thin white blanket. The morning sun was bright, and the big elms dripped with melting snow as I drove to a little Mexican restaurant on Alameda, just west of Broadway. The huevos rancheros were better than average. Hotter, too. Much hotter than any I'd had in Puerto Vallarta. In fact, that was one of the things I'd missed down there, spicy hot food.

Actually, there'd been a lot of things I'd missed. Even the snow. Even the work, come to think of it. Some of it.

I drove to the office. There was a message on my machine from Ed Nylund. He'd found out something about Clare Dickerson and Mr. Rockefeller.

"Two killings," he said after I phoned him. "One murder, one self-defense. I've got some background info, too."

"Tell me."

When Clare Dickerson was sixteen, Ed explained, she ran away from her small hometown and went to the "big city," Kansas City, Missouri. By age seventeen she was working as a hooker. It wasn't long before she was corraled by a pair of pimps, the brothers Washington, Sonny and Maurice, who ran a dozen or so whores in their neighborhood. Clare stayed in their stable for three years.

She was nearly twenty when she met a john named George Rockefeller.

Rockefeller had a wife, two kids, three cars, a small mansion in the suburbs, a stock portfolio worth a quarter of a million dollars, and a raging mid-life crisis.

He tried to ease his troubled mind in the company of young prostitutes, sometimes two at a time. One of those times was with Clare and another woman, who performed on each other and then on him.

Rockefeller was much taken with Clare, or "Holly," as she called herself on the street. He began to see her regularly. She was special—intelligent and beautiful, even under her bleached hair and heavy rouge. More, she desperately wanted off the streets. And Rockefeller wanted a mistress.

They worked it out. He set her up in a nice apartment, bought her clothes and a car, gave her money. He was loaded, no problem. Besides, he'd found ways to write it off on his income tax. Among these were "business trips," where Clare would meet him—New York, Bermuda, Acapulco, Hawaii, Aspen.

In Kansas City, Rockefeller would visit Clare in her apartment. They never went out together, not risking being seen by any of Rockefeller's friends, neighbors, or business associates.

As for Clare, she stayed far away from the street she'd once walked. Still, she always feared someone from the "old days" would see her. But her name was different, and so were her looks. After a while, she relaxed.

This went on for a couple of years.

Then Sonny and Maurice Washington found out that their little lost whore "Holly" was now Miss Goody Two-Shoes Clare Dickerson and was being kept by a rich man.

Sonny and Maurice wanted their cut. Or else, they told her—Holly or Clare or whatever the fuck her name was—they would cut *her*.

Clare was terrified. She considered leaving Kansas City, but where would she go? She'd saved little money, and she had no real friends. Except George Rockefeller.

She told him about the brothers Washington.

He said not to worry, he'd protect her. He bought her a gun. It was cute—a .32 automatic with a chrome finish and mother-of-pearl grips. Clare carried it in her purse. It made her feel safe.

Then, one night, Sonny and Maurice visited her apartment. Sonny picked the lock. He was good at it. Maurice, he was the razor man.

They crept into Clare's bedroom.

George Rockefeller was in bed having sex with Clare.

Clare heard them enter the room. She screamed, pushed Rockefeller off her, and grabbed her purse from the nightstand. Rockefeller took it from her, got the gun out, and put himself between her and the two large men just as Maurice swung his razor.

It caught Rockefeller in the neck, severing his carotid artery. He sank to his knees, firing Clare's gun, hitting Maurice three times, once through the left eye. Sonny ran.

George Rockefeller bled to death before the paramedics could save him.

The entire sordid affair was recounted in the papers for a few days, soon being pushed aside by fresher news—mass murders, gang-style murders, and drug-related murders.

Sonny Washington was arrested and charged with accessory to murder and conspiracy to commit murder. He plea-bargained down to manslaughter and was sentenced to three to five years in the Missouri state prison. After his sentencing, he swore he'd get even for his brother's death.

"He served two years," Ed Nylund said now.

"He's out?"

"He was released on probation last month."

"When last month?"

"Let me see." I heard him shuffle papers. "March fifth."

"Okay, Ed, thanks a lot. I owe you."

Clare Butler's head had been bashed in on March sixteenth, eleven days after Sonny Washington left prison. I wondered if he could've found her that quickly. It was possible.

I phoned Oliver Westfall and told him what I'd just learned. He was pleased with the morbid news.

"I have good contacts in Kansas City," he told me. "I'll have them check out Mr. Washington. With any luck, he wasn't employed or in jail from the fifteenth to the seventeenth of March."

"And if he wasn't?"

"If he has no one but disreputable street people to vouch for his whereabouts, I can present him to the jury and say that *this* man may have murdered Clare Butler."

"Whether or not he did."

He gave me a small but weary sigh. "It doesn't matter whether he killed her. What we're working toward is reasonable doubt in the minds of the jurors. That's all we need to get Mr. Butler acquitted."

Maybe it was my training as a cop, but at this point I was more concerned with who killed Clare than in bullshitting a jury. But I kept it to myself. Westfall was only doing his job.

I asked him, "Do you think Butler knows about Clare's past life in Kansas City?"

He was silent for a moment. "I seriously doubt it."

"So do I. Who gets to tell him?"

"I will, of course. But not every detail, not right away. He's already severely depressed."

"When will you see him?"

"Later this morning."

"Ask him what he knows about Madeline Tate. She was a friend of Clare's and may or may not have information about her secret lover."

"I'll ask him," Westfall said. "In the meantime, there's something I'd like you to do. Question Mr. Butler's neighbors and see if anyone saw a strange vehicle or person that day."

"Haven't the police already done that?"

"Yes, but it can't hurt to double-check."

"Right. By the way, how go the depositions?"

"All three are scheduled for this afternoon."

I was surprised. "Even Winks?"

"Yes. And I must say that when I spoke to him on the phone yesterday, he sounded quite eager to help Mr. Butler. He should be our strongest witness."

"So long as he doesn't talk about alien landings."

Westfall hung up without saying good-bye. I phoned Harvey the mechanic about the condition of the old Olds.

"Not good, Jake. First off, the frame's bent."

"So straighten it."

"It's not that simple."

"Yeah, yeah. What else is wrong?"

He began to list the damaged parts, some I'd never heard of. "It could run as much as two, maybe three—"

"Three hundred? No problem."

"Three thousand."

"*What?*"

"There's a lot of body work. Plus, some of those parts are hard to come by."

"But Jesus Christ, Harvey, three *thousand*?"

"In fact, a lot of the parts on your car, I mean, the undamaged parts, are worth some money."

"You know, my insurance won't cover— What do you mean, 'worth some money'?"

"If we parted it out."

"Chop her up?"

"Exactly. I know I could sell the—"

"Like an organ donor?"

"Come on, Jake. Maybe it's time you bought a new car?"

"A *new* car?"

"Well, it's up to you, of course. You want me to start work on her or not?"

"Christ. Let me think it over."

"Well, call me when you decide. And the loaner, you know I can't let you keep it forever."

"Yeah, yeah."

"You have been adding oil like I told you, right?"

"For chrissake, Harvey, what do you think?" I scribbled a note: *Add oil*.

After I assured Harvey that I'd give him my verdict on the Olds in a day or two, I looked up Madeline Tate in the phone book. There was one "Tate, M." I dialed the number and got an answering machine, a woman's voice that repeated the last four digits I'd dialed and asked me to leave a message. I told her who I was and asked her to please call me if she was the Madeline Tate who'd been acquainted with Clare Butler. I left both my numbers.

If she didn't call by tonight, I'd knock on her door.

In the meantime, I'd have a chat with Christopher Pruitt, Clare Butler's next-to-last lover.

CHAPTER

14

SAMUEL BUTLER HAD TOLD ME THAT Christopher Pruitt
was an agent for Maximum Realty. He hadn't told me
which office, though, and Maximum had them all over
the city.

I called the first one in the phone book. It wasn't the
right office, but they directed me to another number, and
before you could say "commission" I was on the phone
with Pruitt. He sounded friendly enough, but if he knew
why I wanted to see him, he'd probably be "in meetings"
or "showing homes" from now on.

So I used the magic words: "I want to buy a house."

"I'm sure we have just what you're looking for, Mr.
Lomax. What price range did you—"

"Could we do this in your office?"

The building was a four-story brick-and-glass cube just
east of the Cherry Creek shopping center. The center
itself stretched for half a mile along Speer Boulevard. The
east end, the one nearer Maximum's offices, was brand-
new, a bright and shiny complex of shops headed by Saks
Fifth Avenue, Neiman-Marcus, and Lord & Taylor. No
one seemed to notice that the other end, the west end,
was dead—abandoned stores, boarded windows, and
weeds pushing through cracks in the asphalt parking lot.

As the man said, "Don't look back, something might be gaining on you."

Maximum Realty occupied the entire first floor of the building. The waiting area had enough sofas and tables for a soiree. But I was alone, a party of one.

The receptionist announced me on the intercom, and a few minutes later, Christopher Pruitt came out, smiling.

He was around thirty, brown hair and eyes, tall and trim, wearing a navy blue sports coat, khaki slacks, and loafers. You could buy a small car for the price of his thin gold watch. If it was real.

We shook hands, and he led me down the hall past several small conference rooms and a dozen offices, half of them empty. The rest were occupied by men and women persuading clients (on the phone or face-to-face) that the market was improving and this was a *perfect* time to buy—trying not to sound desperate, trying to forget that HUD homes were still coming on the market as fast as the government could sell them, people were leaving the city to find jobs, and in many neighborhoods for-sale signs were as thick as crabgrass. A *tremendous* time to buy.

Pruitt ushered me into his office. I sat in the client's chair. It was beside his desk, not before it, the easier for him to show me photos in the multiple-listing book and shove papers toward me to sign.

"Do you have a price range in mind, Mr. Lomax? Or a particular part of town?"

"No."

"Oh. Well, what *are* you looking for?"

"Information about Clare Butler."

Poor guy. He looked as if I'd punched him in the stomach.

"What?"

"Sorry about the little deception. I'm working for Samuel Butler. I'm a private detective and—"

"Get out of here," Pruitt said, rising.

I remained seated. "Are you trying to hurt my feelings?"

He didn't think that was funny. "I want nothing more to do with Samuel *or* Clare Butler. They've caused me enough grief already. Now get out before I—"

He looked from me to the door to the phone on his desk. He wasn't sure *what* he would do.

"You don't seem too concerned that Clare's dead and Samuel's in jail," I said.

"I'm not. Do I have to call the police?"

"Only if you want to be subpoenaed to the witness stand at Butler's trial and have your dirty little affair with his wife discussed in open court." I had no idea if he'd be called as a witness. But then, neither did he. "You might even make the evening news. That should be a boost for business."

His face was pale, and his hands were clenched in bony fists at his sides.

"Why don't you sit down," I suggested. "We'll talk, and then I'll leave, and you can pretend I was never here."

"I've already been questioned by the police."

"I know. And don't worry, no one thinks you had anything to do with Clare's death."

"What is it you want?"

"Just some information about Clare."

He relaxed enough to sit. But he held the arms of his chair, ready to throw himself to his feet at a moment's notice.

"What information?"

"Let's start with how you and she met."

He shook his head at the memory. "All I did was buy her a drink. Biggest mistake I ever made."

"Where?"

"The Bay Wolf."

I knew the place—a nearby restaurant and jazz lounge. It had been closed for a while, now open under new management. Like a lot of restaurants in Denver.

"When was this?"

"Last November, a week or so before Thanksgiving." He sighed. "The holidays always bring me down. I don't have any family in town. I mean, the reason I moved here from Des Moines was to get *away* from those people. Anyway, I guess around then I spent more time in bars." He sighed again. "She came in one night and sat on the stool next to mine. I bought her and her friend a drink."

"Her friend?"

"Another woman. Damn good-looking. They both were."

"What was her name?"

"I don't remember."

"Madeline Tate?"

He shrugged. "It could've been."

"So you bought them each a drink."

"Right, and before I knew it, Clare's got her hand on my leg. I'm thinking, Thank you, God. We had another round, and then she said she had to leave. Now I'm thinking, Screw you, bitch. Until she asked me if I'd like to meet her for lunch the next day. I said, 'Sure,' and she said, 'Your place.'" Pruitt shook his head again. "If I would've only known . . ."

I waited.

"She came to my town house," he said, "and we had sex. And I mean, she was outstanding." He gave me a knowing look. I gave him nothing back. "Anyway, that's how it started."

"How often did you see her?"

"Two, sometimes three times a week."

"At the Bay Wolf?"

MICHAEL ALLEGRETTO

"No, that was just the first time. From then on we always met at my place."

"How convenient for you."

"Listen," he said heatedly, "*she* was running the show."

"The show?"

Pruitt opened his mouth, then closed it, regaining his composure. "What I meant to say," he said quietly, "meeting at my apartment was her idea."

"Always during the day?"

"Usually, yes. A few times she came to my place at night, but she'd leave early, by eight or so."

"To go home to her husband."

"Hey, she never told me she was married."

I gave him my two-dollar grin. "Why else would she avoid being seen with you?"

"I don't know. . . ." Pruitt looked around his office for an answer. "I suppose I thought it was part of her—"

"Her what?"

He hesitated. "Kinkiness." He pressed his lips together, then said, "I don't see why I have to tell you any of this."

"You don't." I crossed my legs, settled into the chair, and let him know I wasn't about to leave.

He held my gaze for a moment, then looked down at his hands, curling one into a half fist, examining the nails.

After a moment, he said, "She liked bondage." He shrugged. "I'd never done anything like that before. She showed me what to do, how to tie her up. We used some of my old neckties." He fingered the one he had on, then guiltily moved his hand away. "After she was bound, she'd tell me what to do to her, spank her, slap her, push her onto the floor, whatever, then have sex. None of it vicious or hurtful, you understand. It was just play."

96

He frowned, remembering.

"Things changed, though," he said. "Pretty soon she wanted me to hit her. I mean, really hit her. She'd be tied up and telling me slap her, harder, *harder*. If I wouldn't do it, she'd start calling me names, wimp, faggot, whatever, trying to get me mad. And I *would* get mad. And I'd slap her harder . . . and then we'd have sex. It was getting to be too weird, too sick. After about two months, I was ready to call it quits with her. Then her husband found out about us. . . ."

"He put a stop to your affair."

"Oh, that he did," Pruitt said. "He called me at work one day, gave me a phony name, said he was interested in looking at a house that had my name on the for-sale sign. I met him there, we went inside, and he proceeded to beat the hell out of me. He knocked out this tooth"— Pruitt put his finger on a top incisor—"before I covered my head with both arms. He kept hitting me until I fell. He kicked me. I pissed blood for a week. He told me if I ever went near his wife again, he'd kill me. I believed him."

I felt no pity for Pruitt. "Did you go to the police?"

"How could I? What would I say, that a guy beat me up because I was screwing his wife? I didn't tell anyone." He waved his arm. "The people here think I was mugged."

I said nothing.

Pruitt gave me a crooked smile. "Afterward, I wondered if Clare had sensed our affair was ending and sicced her husband on me out of spite."

"When was the beating?"

Pruitt ran his tongue over his front cap. "The first part of January."

"Did you see Clare again after that?"

"Hell no, you think I'm crazy? I *told* you what Butler said."

"Was she seeing anyone else during your affair with her?"

"Not that I know of."

"Did she ever mention another man to you—in any context?"

"No. We didn't talk much while we were together. She'd come over, we'd do our thing, and she'd leave."

"Did you ever do drugs while you were together?"

"*I* didn't."

"Meaning she did?"

"Sometimes."

"Which drugs?"

"Something she smoked in a little glass pipe. She said it made sex better for her."

"Did she ever say where she bought it?"

"I never asked."

"Did the police question you about any of this?"

Pruitt shook his head no. "The only two things they wanted to know were, one, was I still seeing Clare. No. And two, where was I the day she was murdered. San Diego, at a real estate convention. And I've got the credit-card receipts and a dozen witnesses to prove it," he added proudly.

"Lucky for you," I said, standing. "Or you might be learning some real kinkiness in the state pen."

I left him fingering his tie.

I spent the rest of the day going door-to-door in Samuel Butler's neighborhood. At least the sun had come out and mopped up the thin snow, so my feet stayed dry. I asked everyone the same question: Did you see any suspicious-looking vehicles or persons on the day Clare Butler was murdered? They'd all been asked this before by the police. Their answers hadn't changed.

No.

When I got home that evening, the phone was ringing as I came through the door.

"Jacob Lomax?" A man's voice.

"Yes." I tossed my keys on the kitchen counter and got ready to hang up the moment he said "magazine subscriptions" or "carpet cleaning."

He said, "I know who killed Clare Butler."

CHAPTER

15

"WHO IS THIS?"

"A friend," he said. "I have proof that Samuel Butler didn't kill his wife."

I didn't recognize his voice. Not young, not old. Nervous.

"Take it to the police," I told him. I rarely trust people who say they have precisely what I want.

"I can't."

"Why not?"

"It's— They'd arrest me."

"For what?"

"Look, do you want what I have or not?" He was getting exasperated. Tough.

"What exactly do you have?"

"Photographs that can prove who killed Clare Butler. And it wasn't her husband."

"Who was it?"

"You look at the pictures and decide for yourself."

"Okay. I'll leave the porch light on for you."

"No, we'll meet someplace else, someplace where I feel safe. After you see the photos, we'll talk price."

"I don't have much money."

"Samuel Butler does."

"I see." Oddly enough, now I trusted him. At least I trusted his motive. "Okay, when and where?"

"Ten o'clock tonight, Willis Case golf course."

"How about somewhere more public?"

"No way, pal. The cops are looking for me. And so is someone else, someone who wants these photographs."

"Who?"

"The person who killed Clare. Be at the starter's shack at ten." He hung up.

Willis Case golf course is in the northwest part of town, bordered on the south by I-70 and on the other three sides by city streets and residential neighborhoods. I'd often driven past it and seen golfers whaling away at the elusive and hated little white ball, their steel clubs flashing in the sun. Or they'd be stalking said ball, trudging about the hilly, pine-laden grounds, mighty quivers slung from their backs. Others, perhaps fearing sweat, puttered about in motorized carts.

At nine o'clock, I steered the Toyota up the ascending, narrow entrance road, flanked by tall pines. My headlights flashed across the deserted starter's shack and one side of the clubhouse. I continued on to the players' parking lot. It was empty and dark.

I shut off the Toyota and climbed out.

The sky was clear, and the air was cold. The only sounds were the ticking of the Toyota's engine and the distant hum of traffic on the freeway. I turned up my jacket collar, adjusted the holster on my hip, then switched on my flashlight and walked back toward the starter's shack.

The shack abutted one end of the clubhouse, with windows on two sides and a door on the third. All locked. To my left was a garage door, behind which I assumed golf carts were stored.

I moved to my right, stepped over a low metal-pipe railing, and began circling the clubhouse, keeping to the asphalt cart path. I swept my light across the flat, grassy tee box and the tall, dark pines, looking for anyone lurking in the shadows.

There were plenty of places to lurk. The golf course was a two-tone mosaic—dark fairways and black trees. The grounds fell steeply away from the clubhouse to the south and west. In the distance, the mountains were flat, dark shapes against a starry sky. A crescent moon hung over them like a scythe. Through the trees I could see portions of the interstate, a quarter mile away, flowing with traffic.

I continued around the building, peering through the windows. The restaurant was dark save for a single light over the cash register. The empty drawer stuck out like a tongue.

I entered the parking lot from the rear. The Toyota looked lost and abandoned. I moved past it to the starter's shack and clicked off my light.

At least I knew I was alone. No one was lying in ambush or waiting to sneak up on me. Not that I thought there would be. But *something* was making me nervous. Maybe this place. It was a little too dark and a little too remote. Or maybe the enticement itself—a convenient phone call with the promise of the answer to my biggest question. And if the answer was real, photographic evidence of Clare's murderer, why hadn't the mystery man contacted Butler's lawyer or one of his children? Why me?

Unless, of course, the attorney and the kids had been involved in the murder.

The only way to find out was to meet the mystery man. So I stood in the chill night air, shifting my feet and flexing my fingers to stay warm.

An hour later, I heard a car.

It moved slowly in low gear, coming up the entrance

road, invisible behind a thick wall of trees. Then head-lights appeared, at first merely blinking through the branches and finally erupting in full glare as the car rounded the last curve.

I stayed hidden in the shadow beside the starter's shack.

The car stopped about thirty feet from the shack, pas-senger side toward me, nothing between us but a flat stretch of asphalt, a few concrete benches, and spiny bushes that rimmed the road. I could see the dark outline of a man behind the wheel.

"Is that you, Lomax?" he called.

I guess I wasn't so well concealed, after all. I switched on the flashlight and pointed it at the car. A new Thun-derbird, dark, hard to tell the color in the pale yellow beam of the flash. The man behind the wheel was partially hidden by the doorframe, but I could see that he was heavyset, middle-aged or older.

"It's me," I told him.

"Come over to the car."

I took two steps forward.

Someone rose from the backseat and pointed something at me, and I dove to the ground.

In the next instant there was a flash and a boom, and the starter's shack window exploded behind me in a shower of glass. I rolled under the pipe railing as a power-ful beam of light fell on me. Two booms, close together. Lead shot splattered into the asphalt and the brick build-ing. I scrambled on all fours, then ran in a crouch around the corner of the clubhouse.

From behind me I heard, "You two go that way. I'll drive around the other side."

Three of them. At least two had shotguns. I didn't know Who or Why, but I knew What, Where, and When—kill me, here and now.

I considered breaking into the building through a window and making my stand inside. But there were too many ways in, too many entries to defend. Besides, there wasn't time. They were running now. They'd blast me before I climbed halfway in.

I ran past the end of the clubhouse. To my left was the parking lot. A car door slammed.

I reached the end of the cart path. Beyond it was a short stretch of grass that fell away in a steep slope. I heard the action of a pump shotgun behind me, and I dove forward as a tight bundle of lead slugs tore the air over me. I rolled twenty feet downhill and landed with my face in the sand. The night-blackened green stretched before me. Beyond it, the ground dropped into the pines. To my right, past the front of the green, the grass sloped down to a wide open fairway.

I was still holding the flashlight, and it was still on. I heaved it to my right.

"There!"

A boom.

I scrambled out of the sand trap, ran across the green, and stumbled down the slope into the trees.

"No, there he goes!"

A boom.

Slugs smashed into the trees, stinging me with bits of bark and wood. I dodged through the pines, slipping on the bed of needles. Branches grabbed my coat and slapped my face.

Suddenly, I was in the open.

The ground sloped gently down from me across the width of another fairway, then up to a distant, high chain-link fence. Beyond the fence was the interstate, with cars and trucks humming along in a thin but continuous stream. Between me and the fence was about fifty yards of open ground, stretching both ways parallel to the traffic. It was doubtful I could run that far without being cut down from behind. And if I *did* make it across and if I *could* scale the fence, then what? Run headlong into sixty-mile-an-hour traffic?

I heard the crunch of needles behind me. They'd entered the pines.

I faced in their direction, backing into the open, scanning the island of trees. It was about twenty yards deep and stretched fifty yards to either side of me. I figured the driver was coming toward me from the right and the other two from straight ahead.

I moved to my left, dodging from tree to tree, keeping my back in the open and as much timber as possible between me and the shooters. After a dozen yards, I stopped and listened, quietly unholstering the .38, wishing it were an Uzi, wishing more that I'd stayed in Mexico. I saw movement in the trees, shadows among shadows. One stopped and turned toward me, a man-shape twenty feet away. I pointed the snub-nose and popped off three rounds, knowing my odds of hitting anything at that distance were slim. I was answered at once by gunfire, thundering booms interspersed with sharper cracks. I hugged the base of a tree under a shower of pinecones and ripped bark.

Someone moaned. I held my breath and hoped it wasn't me.

"Shit, Royce is hit."

"Forget about Royce. Let's get that son of a bitch."

I started moving again to my left, dodging in the dark from tree to tree.

Then I reached the tip of my island. Not quite ahead of me, at an upward angle to my left, was the elevated green. About fifty yards beyond it was the clubhouse, the top half of its windows peeking over the slope at me. Directly ahead of me was the stand of trees, angling in on me from both sides like the tip of a giant spear.

The two able-bodied shooters crunched through the pine needles, working their way toward me.

Their friend Royce may have been careless, perhaps believing I was unarmed. But these two knew better. They'd pinned me with my back to the fairway, and they were about to flush me into the open. There was no out-gunning them, so I turned, prepared to run and take my chance as a moving target in the open fairway.

Then I hesitated, thinking about the clubhouse windows. Something I should have thought of before.

I turned and held the .38 before me with both hands. I fired my two remaining rounds at the distant, dark building, praying for a miracle.

I got one.

Glass shattered, and the night came alive with the clang of a burglar alarm.

"Goddammit," I heard through the clanging.

"What if it's tied to a cop station?"

"God *damn* it. All right. Let's get the fuck out of here."

"Help me with Royce."

"Forget about him. He's finished."

"We can't just—"

Three sharp gunshots. I hunkered down behind my tree.

"Jesus Christ."

"Come on."

Movement in the trees. Then two shapes ran across the green and up the slope, disappearing over the top. A few moments later, an engine roared, and tires squealed. The engine raced off in the night.

The alarm continued its steady clang.

I listened for Royce. He'd stopped moaning.

I waited a good five minutes before I left the trees and began hunting for my flashlight. It was still switched on, lying in the fairway. I carried it back into the trees.

Royce was lying on his back in a bed of pine needles. He was a husky guy, my age or older, late thirties, with long hair and a bandido mustache. He wore Levi's and a black crew-neck sweater. His eyes and mouth were open, as if he'd just made a hole in one. Actually, there were four holes, glistening with blood.

I climbed the grassy slope to the clubhouse and waited for the cops.

CHAPTER

16

I SPENT THE NIGHT in the city jail.

It wasn't too surprising, since a man had been shot dead and I'd been the only one around with a gun. Except, of course, for the uniformed officers.

They'd arrived a few minutes after I reached the clubhouse, two men and a woman in three white patrol cars—lights out, sirens mute, tires squealing. The loudest sound was the clanging of the alarm bell. I stood in plain view away from the building and waved both arms in the air to show them I was a responsible citizen. Still, they felt it prudent to point their weapons at me.

I gave them the short version: I was a private detective meeting an informant, and three guys had driven up and tried to kill me, so I'd shot one of them, then shot the window, setting off the alarm.

They took my gun and walked me down to the trees to the body. Then they put me in the backseat of a patrol car and called for Homicide. After that, detectives and technicians swarmed the place, photographing the body and searching for the dead man's gun. None was found.

The detectives asked me a lot of questions. I'd answered most of them.

The others, I told them, were privileged information. They said, "Okay," and then took me downtown. I told them I wanted to talk to Lt. Patrick MacArthur, a close personal friend of mine. They said, "Fine," and then had me pictured and printed. I told them MacArthur and I had been cops together, had in fact gone through the academy together. They said, "Swell," and then locked me up.

I slept very little that night.

I have that problem in a strange bed. Particularly if it's a narrow cot surrounded by concrete and steel. There were other distractions—steel doors clanging, toilets flushing, guys yelling. And when I did nod off, I kept having the same dream: men with shotguns were chasing me through the trees.

At ten o'clock Thursday morning a detective let me out of my cell and took me upstairs.

He was an Oriental named O'Roarke. We'd met some months ago under equally distressing conditions, but he acted as if he'd never seen me before in his life. He was the silent type. In fact, he didn't say a word as we went up the elevator, then walked through the busy squad room to a glass-paneled door in the back. On the door was stenciled Robbery/Homicide Section—Lt. P. MacArthur. I could see MacArthur going through some papers on his desk. O'Roarke knocked. MacArthur looked up and waved us in.

"Jake," he said by way of greeting.

He motioned me into a chair facing his desk. I sat. O'Roarke closed the door and stood in silence behind me.

"I see you still like to sleep in your clothes," MacArthur said.

"Is that why they didn't serve me breakfast?"

"Have some coffee."

He took the glass pot from his coffee machine and poured me a cup. His movements were clean and precise. So were his clothes: tailored gray-and-white houndstooth suit, off-white shirt, maroon silk jacquard tie with a floral print. He was a year younger than I, but I felt as if he were the school principal and I had been summoned to his office for fighting in the playground. Maybe it was my grass-stained pants and the dirt in my hair.

"The dead man's name is William Royce." MacArthur leaned over his desk to hand me the cup. "Do you know him?"

"Nope." I sipped the coffee. It could've been stronger, but at least it cut the foul taste in my mouth.

"We ran him through NCIC," MacArthur said, turning a page on his desk. "He's got a list of priors, all in California, mostly assaults, some drug related. He did six years in San Quentin for second-degree murder. We think he's probably a low-rate killer for hire."

"Lucky for me he wasn't the expensive kind."

MacArthur said, "Mmm," and turned another page. "By the way, do you own a nine-millimeter automatic?"

"I own revolvers."

"No automatics?"

"Call me old-fashioned."

"Mmm-hmm." MacArthur tapped a paper with a manicured nail. "Autopsy report. I had them rush it first thing this morning. Royce had one thirty-eight slug in his abdomen and three nine-millimeter slugs in his chest. One of those punctured his heart. That's what killed him, so you're probably off the hook."

"Imagine my relief."

"We found nine-millimeter and twelve-gauge shell casings at the scene. No guns."

"Royce had a pump-action shotgun, and so did one of the others. The third guy, the driver, must've had the automatic. Obviously, they took Royce's gun with them."

MacArthur was reading a typed form on his desk, acting as if it were important and I wasn't. What the hell, maybe I wasn't. I mean, he and I *used* to be close friends, but that had been a long time ago. We'd been cops together. His wife had introduced me to Katherine, whom I'd married. And when Katherine had been murdered, MacArthur had helped me get back on my feet again. In fact, now that I thought about it, *he'd* gotten me started in this so-called profession. So in a way, it was his fault that I'd nearly been blown away last night. But I'm sure he had other things on his mind. For instance, the next rung up the bureaucratic ladder. The top spot in the Crimes Against Persons Bureau was soon to be vacated. A captain's post. If—I mean, *when* MacArthur got promoted, I'd probably never see him again, except occasionally on the nightly news.

"Some friend," I said.

He looked up. "Excuse me?"

"Nothing."

Now he regarded me with cool gray eyes. "There are a few blanks in these reports, things you refused to tell the detectives. Like why exactly you were at a golf course in the middle of the night."

"Trying to correct my slice?"

He didn't smile. He used to smile.

"As I told the detectives, I was meeting an informant."

"What's his name?"

"I only spoke to him on the phone, and he didn't identify himself."

"But he had *something* for you."

"He said he had photographs that proved Samuel Butler didn't murder his wife."

"Samuel Butler," MacArthur repeated, raising one eyebrow. "What's your interest in him?"

"I'm working for him. That is, for his attorney, Oliver Westfall."

Now both eyebrows went up, crinkling his forehead. "You must sorely need money to work for a murderer."

"You mean accused murderer."

111

"I mean murderer. His prints were on the wrench."

"Naturally. It was his wrench. But the prints were partially smudged. Someone wearing gloves could have—"

"Butler killed her, Jake. Learn to live with it."

I said nothing. I could've reminded him that a man was innocent until proven guilty in a court of law, but it would be wasted breath on MacArthur. Like most cops, he felt that if there was enough evidence to bring a man to trial, then he was guilty, period. If he was found "not guilty" by a jury, it didn't mean he hadn't committed the crime; it just meant he'd beaten the system.

MacArthur leaned back in his chair and made a steeple of his fingers. He tipped it down and pointed it at me.

"These photographs were a ruse to set you up," he said.

"Obviously."

"There are no photographs."

"Probably not."

"The question is why did these men want to kill you?"

"I have no idea."

"Who have you pissed off lately?"

"No one. I've been lying on the beach in Mexico for the past few months."

"Not with someone's wife, I hope."

I let that pass.

So did he. He asked, "Do you think there's a connection with Samuel Butler?"

"It's possible."

"Like what?"

"If I tell you, will you promise not to laugh?"

He said nothing.

"Maybe Samuel Butler is innocent and the real killer is worried, now that I'm on the case."

He blew air between tight lips.

I changed the subject. "Why do you suppose they killed Royce?"

MacArthur shrugged. "You'd seriously wounded him.

112

Apparently they didn't want to carry him or leave him behind to talk."

"Some friends."

He cocked an eyebrow at me and then dropped it into a frown. When he spoke, there was concern in his voice—professional, nothing to do with friendship.

"Are you positive you don't know who these guys are?"

I'd just told him who I thought they were, but he didn't want to hear it. "I'm sure."

"Or why they'd want to kill you. Besides this supersleuth fantasy."

"No."

He held my eyes a moment longer, then flipped a few more pages on his desk. "I guess we're finished for now. We'll have to hold your gun for a ballistics check. And you'll probably get a bill in the mail."

I stood. "A bill for what?"

"You broke a window in the clubhouse. That's private property."

"You've got to be kidding."

He wasn't. "And if I were you, I'd think twice before meeting any more strangers in dark places."

"Thanks for the tip."

I turned to go, then gave a start when I saw O'Roarke standing behind me. He'd been so quiet I'd forgotten he was there.

He spoke for the first time. "Jumpy?"

I liked him better when he was silent.

A taxi took me from the police building to the golf course, where the Toyota was hidden in a crowd of cars. The day was overcast, heavy with the smell of spring rain, but there were plenty of golfers wandering the fairways and milling about the starter's shack.

I paid the cabby and walked to the shack. The guy inside didn't look too happy. Maybe because his front window had been replaced with a plywood board. Likewise a window on the side of the clubhouse, the one I'd shot out.

I moved aside to let a foursome in two golf carts buzz by, then walked past the clubhouse to the top of the grassy slope. Below me, on the eighteenth green, four grown men in red and yellow pants putted and missed and groaned. Life's tough.

Beyond them were the trees where William Royce had been shot to death.

I considered walking down there, but what would be the point? There was nothing to search for. The police had already scoured the area and collected all the "clues"—empty shells and one dead body. Besides, I wasn't looking for clues. I was looking for answers.

Why had Royce and company tried to kill me? It was almost certainly connected with Clare Butler's murder, because that was my only case. And the mystery caller knew I was on it. Had I already met Clare's killer without realizing it? Or was he trying to make sure that I didn't meet him? Either way, it now looked like Clare's death was more than the violent end of a lovers' quarrel. I'd have to watch my back from now on. Assuming I stayed on the case.

As opposed to what? Drop everything and run back to Mexico?

I walked toward the parking lot.

The rain beat me there.

CHAPTER

17

I DROVE HOME IN A THUNDERSTORM.

This is what they mean by "springtime in the Rockies." Rain, snow, hail, sunshine—sometimes all in the same day. Although today it looked like the rain would hang on for a while.

When I turned onto my block, I found it lined with parked cars, so I had to leave the Toyota around the corner. By the time I jogged to the old mansion, my clothes were soaked, and my hair was plastered to my head.

Mrs. Finch greeted me at the front door.

"Where do you think you're going?" she snapped. She wore a navy blue dress with tiny white dots—long sleeves, high collar, low hemline. Her little fists were on her hips, and her head was cocked to one side. She looked up at me like a terrier eyeing a mailman.

"I, uh, thought I'd go up to my apartment."

"Not dripping wet, you're not. Not across my carpet that I had shampooed this very morning, no, sir." She snapped one hand off her hip to point at the ancient, floral-patterned carpet behind her.

"Well, what do—"

"You just stand right there, mister."

She turned on her heel and marched through her open apartment door. I dripped on the welcome mat, stared at the empty entry hall, and wondered if Mrs. Finch expected me to stay there until I was dry. But no, she'd left her door open. And sure enough, a minute later she came bustling out, her mouth grim, a bath towel in her hand. She threw it at me.

"Thank—"

"Dry your hair and take off your shoes before you even *think* about tromping upstairs." She stomped back to her apartment, then turned in the open doorway and shook a crooked finger at me. "And why don't you find *real* work. Something that doesn't keep you out till all hours of the night."

"I—"

"And buy an umbrella!" she shouted, slamming her door.

Mrs. Finch likes to look after her tenants.

Upstairs, I undressed in the bathroom and threw my clothes in a heap in the corner. I let the shower's hot spray wash off the cold rain and the stale stink of jail. It also eased the stiffness in my back from rolling around on the ground last night. Mrs. Finch was wrong; this *was* real work.

I toweled off and put on sweats and running shoes—not that I'd be running. I was tired and hungry. Mostly tired, so I stretched out on the couch for a quick nap. I fell asleep to the sound of the rain.

When I awoke, the apartment was silent. The rain had stopped.

I guess I'd been more tired than I'd thought; my watch said it was nearly five. My neck was stiff from sleeping in one position for too long, so I did twenty minutes of bends and stretches on the living-room floor. Then I walked out through the kitchen to the back balcony.

The air had the clean, fresh smell that only comes after a rain.

The spring storm had passed over the city and moved

to the southeast, where the sky was black and ominous. Overhead there were gray shreds of clouds and patches of blue. The yard below was in shadow. But the tops of the trees glistened, their new, wet leaves clinging hopefully to the bright, dying sun.

I went inside and fixed dinner—a six-egg omelet with ham, onion, mushrooms, and salsa. Then I put on a sports coat and slacks, holster and Magnum.

The gun felt like a brick under my arm. There was no avoiding it, though. The cops had my smaller gun, and I wasn't about to continue with this case unarmed. Three guys had tried to kill me, and two were still out there. I figured if I kept poking into Clare Butler's past life, the shooters would find me again. I hoped I'd be prepared when they showed up.

I phoned Oliver Westfall to see if he'd asked Butler about Clare's friend Madeline Tate. His office was closed for the day.

I drove to my office. I went up the stairs slowly, hand on the butt of my gun. The pals of the dead man Royce no doubt knew I kept this place. Not a bad spot for an ambush.

But the hallway was empty.

So was my office.

The message light on my machine was blinking in sets of three. I pushed the button, and the tape rewound and played them in order.

Number 1: "This is Oliver Westfall. We have a problem. Call me at your earliest convenience." Since he hadn't given me his unlisted home number, I'd have to wait until tomorrow.

Number 2: "Jake, it's Harvey. Have you made a decision about your Olds?" I had not.

Number 3: "Mr. Lomax, this is Madeline Tate returning your call. It's six o'clock, Wednesday night. I . . . well, call me again if you like."

It was now six-thirty, Thursday. I dialed her number. She answered on the second ring.

"Ms. Tate? This is Jacob Lomax."

"Oh. Hello." She sounded cautious.

"Thanks for calling me back," I said. "I assume, then, that you knew Clare Butler."

"I did. I . . . it was horrible what happened."

"Yes, it was. As I said in my message, I'm working for Mr. Butler's attorney, and I'd like to ask you some questions about Clare."

"We were only casual friends. I'm not sure how much I can tell you."

"Anything would be a help. Can we meet somewhere?"

"Do you mean now? I just got home from work."

I waited.

After a moment, she said, "Why don't you give me half an hour and then come here."

"That would be fine."

Dahlia Lane was a short, circular street only a few miles east of the Butler residence. It looked wet and clean after the heavy rain. So did Madeline Tate's frame ranch, which had been built in the fifties, when carports were in. There was a three-year-old Volkswagen Jetta in the semidarkness near the front door. Ms. Tate hadn't left a light on for me. I parked the Toyota in the street, walked up the driveway, and rang the bell.

A dog barked. A big one, by the sound of him. He shut up just before the porch light went on and the door opened.

"Mr. Lomax?"

"Yes."

"Please come in."

Madeline Tate was an attractive woman on my side of thirty, with violet eyes and ash-blond hair that fell in tight curls to her shoulders. She wore a short, shapely tan skirt and a cream-colored blouse with long sleeves and padded shoulders. We were at eye level with each other until I took the one step up into the house.

"Don't mind Tobey," she said.

Tobey was the ugliest rottweiler in the state, and he knew it. He scowled at me, daring me to make a wise-crack about his looks, every muscle tense, from his broad muzzle to his thick, stubby tail.

"Cute dog."

Tobey growled.

"Tobey, no."

Madeline led me through the small entryway. On the right was a large white kitchen with a stone-tiled floor. To the left, a hallway pointed toward the bedrooms. I followed her into the living room, picking up faint traces of her perfume. Paloma Picasso. Tobey grumbled at my heels.

"Please sit down," she said, and motioned me to the couch.

She sat in an armchair, putting the glass-topped coffee table between us. There were tasteful prints on the walls and a floor lamp in the corner that filled the room with soft light. It was all very pleasant, but I had the feeling that something was not quite right, something was missing.

"I was shocked when I heard about Clare," she said.

I nodded. "Were you two close?"

"I wouldn't say 'close.' As I told you on the phone, we were casual friends. We'd meet once every few weeks for lunch or to go shopping. Tobey, lie down."

The thick-bodied brute had been standing beside her chair, staring at me across the glass tabletop, gauging the distance between his jaws and my Adam's apple. Now he snorted at me and flopped down on the carpet.

"When did you and Clare first meet?" I asked.

"About a year ago. On a cruise ship. My . . . husband

119

and I had the cabin next to theirs. It was really quite a coincidence when we later discovered that we *lived* near them, too."

That's what I'd felt was missing—the husband. This house was too big for one person.

"Are you recently divorced?"

She frowned with her eyes and smiled with her mouth. "Does it show?"

"Only to the highly trained detective." I held up my left hand. "No ring."

"Separated," she said matter-of-factly. "The divorce will be final next month." She unconsciously rubbed the underside of her ring finger with her thumb, as if the ring had left a phantom pain, like an amputated limb. "Brian and I never should've gotten married in the first place. 'Irreconcilable differences,' they call it." She smiled without humor, staring into the middle distance. "I call it 'he turned out to be a jerk.' Maybe I was just blinded by the romance, the wine and roses and candlelight dinners. Still, I felt I knew him when we got married, knew the kind of man he was—kind and caring. Well, all he cared about was himself. I was one of his possessions."

I said nothing.

She shook her head, returning from her tangent. "But we were talking about Clare."

"Right. You met on a cruise ship."

"Yes."

"Did the four of you get together after the cruise?"

"No. Neither my husband nor I cared much for Samuel Butler. He was a crude, loud-mouthed bore." She pressed her lips together. "I still can't believe he murdered her."

"He may not have."

"But the police . . ."

"The police are convinced he did it. But there's some evidence to the contrary."

"Well, if not him . . . then who?"

"That's what I'm trying to find out. Butler seems to think Clare was having an affair and that her lover ended her life. So far, I haven't learned who the lover was."

Madeline looked away from me and chewed her bottom lip. There was a lot of it to chew.

I asked, "Do you know who she was seeing?"

"The only one I knew about for sure was Christopher Pruitt. But that was months ago."

"I've met him. A terrific individual. They broke up when Butler learned of the affair."

Madeline nodded. She did not look happy.

"Clare told me about that affair when it started," she said. "She told me it was therapy."

"Therapy?"

Madeline gave me a crooked smile. "Clare made it clear to me that the only reason she married Butler was his money. But she also wanted an active sex life. And according to her, Butler was—if you'll pardon the expression—a 'bum fuck.' "

"I see."

"Also, Pruitt wasn't the only one she saw during that time. There were others." She made a face. "Quickies, she called them. You see, I'd recently separated from my husband, and Clare said I should get out of the house, meet some men. So I went with her to a few nightclubs. I'd never really cared for that scene, but I *did* need to get out of the house. Except it was Clare who always picked up a man, and I'd go home alone. Which was fine with me. Once she even suggested . . ."

"What?"

She smiled with one side of her mouth. "Clare was adventuresome. One time, after she'd met some guy, she proposed that we make it a threesome."

"Oh?"

"Of course I declined."

"Of course. Not counting these one-night stands, was she seeing anyone at the time of her death?"

"Well . . . she never said so, but I got the impression that she was."

"How's that?"

"Her attitude seemed different. I mean, she'd get pretty stressed out when she talked about Samuel, but otherwise she seemed, well, satisfied."

"I see. Could it have had anything to do with drugs?"

"No. I mean I never saw Clare do drugs."

"Did she ever mention one called ice?"

"Ice?" Madeline frowned and shook her head. Then she looked away, her delicate eyebrows still scrunched together.

"What is it?"

"I was thinking about one of Clare's men," she said, "one she'd been looking for."

"Looking for? You mean another bar pickup?"

"No, I believe this was something else, something more. What she said was, let's see, how did she put it— this man would be her 'ticket out of here.' "

" 'Out of here' meaning . . . ?"

"Out of Denver. Out of her life with Samuel Butler."

"Could this be the person who was 'satisfying' her?"

"It's possible. The time was the same, a few months ago."

"If she was satisfied, then she must've found him."

"Yes, I suppose so. If it was the same man."

"And you're sure you don't know his name?"

"Clare never said. But I know she was trying very hard to find him. She even hired a private eye."

"She did? Who?"

Madeline shrugged her shoulders and shook her head. "I'm sorry, I don't— Although . . ." She tapped a tapered, unpainted nail on her top right incisor. "Although she did say hiring this man was poetic justice."

"Meaning what?"

"It was the same private eye who'd found out about Pruitt. The one Butler had hired to spy on *her*."

CHAPTER

18

I KNEW THE INVESTIGATOR'S NAME—Gil Lucero. When I'd interviewed Butler in jail, he'd said Lucero was "one of the best." I hoped he was right. If so, I might be near the end of my search.

I asked Madeline for her phone books.

There was no Lucero in the yellow pages under DETECTIVE AGENCIES or INVESTIGATORS. Under "Lucero" in the white pages there were five "G's," four "Gilberts," and one "Gilroy."

"Would you like to use the phone?"

"This could take some time. I'd better do it somewhere else." I stood. "I want to thank you for—"

"I have coffee," she said, standing, raising her brows above her incredibly violet eyes. "That is, if you'd like to stay."

"Thanks just the same, but I really should make the calls."

"That's what I mean."

"Oh."

"It's, well, I'd like to help. No, that sounds stupid. But I want to contribute something. Clare wasn't exactly my dearest friend, but in many ways she was dear. And despite her . . . extracurricular activities, I liked her. It's horrible that she died. The way she died. And if, as you say, Samuel Butler didn't kill her, then—"

"I said he may not have killed her."

"May not." She gave a small shrug. "Anyway, I feel sorry for him."

"Samuel?"

"Yes."

Before I could ask why, she said, "The phone's in the kitchen."

I followed her there and sat at a small, round oak table in what I supposed was called "the breakfast nook." Madeline laid out place mats, cups, and saucers. Tobey and I watched her every move. She seemed a bit nervous, as if she weren't accustomed to having a man here after dark. She removed a glass pot from a sleek machine on the counter and poured. Tobey lay down on the floor beside her chair, facing me, staying within striking distance.

I began calling Luceros.

Out of ten possibilities I got six definite noes, two busy signals, one answering machine, and one disconnect. Madeline and I sipped coffee and waited for the busy signals to clear.

"You said you felt sorry for Samuel Butler."

"Yes."

"Why?"

"Well, if he's been wrongly accused—"

"Aside from that."

She set down her cup and brushed a stray curl from her cheek with the back of her fingers.

"He idolized Clare," she said. "And she slept around behind his back. No one deserves that." She glanced away and added bitterly, "No one."

I supposed she'd had a similar experience. I was sure when she forced a smile and completely changed the subject: "How does one get to be a private detective?"

"Would you like to apply?"

Her smile became real. "No, thanks. I'm content being an architect."

"And how does one get to be an architect?"

"By choosing parents with enough money to put me through six years of college. But you haven't answered my question."

"Sorry," I said. "I'm better at asking than answering. Let's see, how does one become a private detective? In my case, first I was a public one."

"A cop."

"We prefer the term *policeman*."

"No doubt," she said with a grin. "Did you quit or—"

"I quit."

"Why?" she asked, and then my look must've changed, because she added quickly, "I'm sorry, I didn't mean to pry."

"You're not. It's, ah, I had a bad experience. I guess I lost my enthusiasm for police work. For team work."

"Oh."

She wasn't about to ask, but she wanted to know more. Or maybe I just felt like telling her. Test the old wound, see if it still hurt.

"My wife was murdered," I said, "and her killers were never caught." There, now that wasn't so bad. Although Madeline was looking at me as if I'd just spilled coffee in my lap. Or in hers. "It's not that I blamed the police for not getting them," I said, not wanting to stop, maybe not able to. "It was a random murder. Or I should say Katherine was a random victim, because the killers were definitely after *somebody*. They just didn't care who. Three of them. They grabbed her in a supermarket parking lot in broad daylight. There were even witnesses, not that it mattered. Two men, they said, and a third person driving their late-model car. Out-of-state plates. That was it."

Madeline was staring at me, not moving, not speaking.

"They found her body a few days later in a ditch east of the city," I said, listening to my voice, searching for the slightest quaver, finding none. "She'd been beaten and raped and stabbed and— Well, anyway, I was a mess for a while, went a little crazy, stopped being a cop. I guess the worst part was having to admit that these guys would never be caught, at least not for *this* crime."

Madeline hesitated. "That couldn't have been the worst part."

"What do you mean?" My voice was loud enough to make Tobey raise his head from his paws. This was *my* wound. Who was she to tell me anything about it?

"The worst part was that you lost your wife."

"I know that," I said sharply.

Tobey growled. Madeline dropped her hand to his head.

"I'm . . . sorry," I said. "Of course, you're right. Anyway, that was a long time ago, five years this June. I'm over it now."

"Are you?"

"Sure." Maybe I *like* living alone and having very few friends and not being able to sustain a relationship with a woman for more than a month. "Sure I am."

She opened her mouth to speak, then closed it. There may have been sadness in her eyes, but I refused to recognize it.

She asked me quietly, "Would you like more coffee?"

"No. I'm sorry, I mean, yes. Please."

In only a few minutes our conversation had gone from Samuel and Clare Butler to Katherine. Why had I opened up to this woman, this stranger?

Before I'd gone to Mexico, I hadn't thought much about Katherine, not consciously, anyway. Sometimes a bad dream. That was it. But in Mexico I'd thought about her a lot, about our life together, about my life after her. I was still influenced by her. No, not by her—by my own sense of loss.

An odd image came to mind, an East Indian monkey trap—a wide-bodied, narrow-necked vase with pieces of coconut in the bottom. A monkey would reach in and grab a fistful of coconut and try to pull it out. His fist wouldn't fit through the narrow neck. He'd be trapped. Of course, all he had to do was let go of the coconut and he could free himself. But he was too stupid to let go. If he could only let go . . .

Maybe that was the reason for my occupational crisis, or whatever the hell it was. I was trying to let go. But I was letting go of the wrong thing.

Madeline poured us coffee, and I phoned the two "busy" Gil Luceros.

This time they were both free. The second one was my man.

After I introduced myself, he said, "Westfall told me you were my stand-in."

"Only until you're back on your feet."

"I'm on them now," he said. "With crutches. So what's up? You didn't call to socialize."

"I need your help. Clare Butler hired you to find someone, and I need to know his name. And if you found him, of course."

Lucero was silent for a moment. "Normally, I wouldn't reveal that information unless I had permission from my client."

"Who happens to be dead."

He was silent a moment longer.

"I don't want to talk about this on the phone," he said. "I'll come to you."

He gave me his address, then added, "And bring some ID."

I hung up. "I have to go."

"Oh. Okay."

"I'm sorry to be abrupt."

"No, it's okay. I understand."

She walked me to the door.

"Thanks for the use of your phone."

"You're welcome."

"I, ah, look, I'm sorry I made you listen to this stuff about my wife and all. I mean, here I am a stranger in your house and I'm unloading my morbid emotional baggage—"

"Please don't apologize. Or I'll have to."

"Excuse me?"

"I unloaded first, remember?"

"Well, now that you mention it. So I guess we're even."

"Even," she said, and smiled faintly. "Good night."

I walked out to my car. The porch light stayed on until I'd driven away.

CHAPTER

19

GIL LUCERO WAS HURTING. I could see it in his eyes.

He was an average-sized guy, around fifty, a bit hunched over because of the crutches. His round face was a pale shade of brown, and his hair and mustache were neatly trimmed, both once black, now mostly gray. He wore a baggy red sweat suit and worn-out slippers. He checked my driver's license at the door, as if this were a nightclub and I might be underage.

"You take a lousy picture," he said, handing it back.

"Who doesn't."

He turned from me, wincing, and hobbled into the living room. There was an overstuffed couch and a couple of matching armchairs, one of which had been dragged to the picture window. The blinds were open, and the chair faced the night. I could see lights scattered in Washington Park, six floors down and across the street. Beside the chair was an end table with a pair of binoculars and a glass half-filled with amber liquid. A way to pass the time. Gil Lucero had been homebound for too long.

He gritted his teeth, eased himself onto one end of the couch, and laid the crutches at his side. He let out his breath.

"Goddamn legs," he said. "I have more stainless steel and Teflon in them than I have in my kitchen."

I sat in the opposing chair.

He asked, "How did you find out Clare Butler hired me?"

"From her friend. Madeline Tate."

He nodded. "I remember her. Good-looking woman. I spotted her and Clare together a few times when I was watching Clare."

"For Samuel Butler."

"Right." He winced and rubbed his right leg. "I don't generally take on that kind of work, the suspicious spouse and so on. The money's good, but there's too much pain involved. On both sides. You know what I'm saying?"

"Absolutely."

"But I do a lot of work for Westfall, and when he asked me to help Butler, well . . . as I said, the money's good." He winced again, then gritted his teeth and swung his legs up on the couch. He let out his breath, saying, "Son of a bitch."

"Can I get you anything?"

"My drink, if you don't mind."

I retrieved his half-full glass from the table by the window.

"You might put in some more bourbon and a couple of cubes."

"No problem."

There was a wet bar at the end of the room. I fixed up Lucero's drink. Then I made myself one.

"Appreciate it," he said when I handed him his glass.

I sat in my chair.

"So," he said.

"Who did Clare Butler want you to find?"

"A guy named Jeremy Stone."

"Did you?"

"Find him? No. But I barely started looking before *this* happened." He nodded at his legs. "Are you thinking Stone was connected with Clare's death?"

"Well, somebody killed her, and I don't think it was
Butler."

We drank our bourbons. Macho private eyes. All we
needed were a couple of dames to oil our .45s.

"Why not Butler?"

I explained how he'd spent the afternoon of his wife's
death, not exactly like a man who'd just committed
murder.

"Butler believes Clare was having an affair," I said.
"The night before her death, he'd overheard her arguing
with someone on the phone. A 'lovers' quarrel' is how he
described it. Maybe this Stone was the lover."

"Maybe . . ." He sounded doubtful. "Clare never said
exactly why she wanted me to find this guy, but I got the
impression it was about money, not love."

"What did she tell you about him?"

Lucero said Clare had come to him about six weeks
ago, around the middle of February. The first thing she'd
asked him was could he work for her and not tell her
husband.

"I told her sure, but if she was worried about that, why
not hire another investigator?"

Clare said it was because she "enjoyed the irony." She
told Lucero the only things she knew about Jeremy Stone
were his name and that he was connected with Butler
Manufacturing Company—but whether as an employee,
a customer, or a supplier, she had no idea. Lucero asked
how she'd learned of Stone. She was reluctant to say.
Lucero pressed the point, wanting as much information
as possible. Finally, Clare said she'd heard the name from
a salesclerk in a boutique, who'd heard it from Kenneth
Butler's wife, Doreen. She would say no more. She told
Lucero it was crucial that neither Kenneth nor Doreen
learn she was looking for Jeremy Stone.

"Did she say why?" I asked.

"No."

"Did you talk to the salesclerk?"

Lucero nodded. "She was the first person I questioned. Works at an upscale boutique in Cherry Creek, a place frequented by Clare. Apparently, Doreen occasionally shopped there, but never lavishly. That changed some months ago, when Doreen began going in there practically every week to buy a couple of dresses or sweaters or whatever. She said something in passing to this clerk, something about 'being able to splurge, now that Jeremy Stone was involved in her husband's business.' "

Lucero shrugged. "That was it. That's all I had to go on. I started hanging out at a bar near Butler Manufacturing. Some of Butler's employees drop in there after work, and I was hoping to get close to one or two of them. But then I had the accident." He winced, whether from the memory or the pain, I couldn't tell.

"You never found out anything about Jeremy Stone?"

"No. I asked a few employees, but they'd never heard of him. At least that's what they said."

"Which bar?"

He told me. "But if I were you, assuming you're going to look for Stone . . ."

"Which I am."

"Then I'd start somewhere else."

"With Kenneth and Doreen Butler."

Lucero nodded. "That's where I would've gone first if Clare hadn't specifically told me not to."

I finished my bourbon and stood. "Thanks for the information. And the drink."

He nodded, then swung his legs off the couch, grimacing.

"Don't get up," I said. "I can find my way out."

"Okay."

"By the way, what happened?"

"This?" He rubbed his legs. "I was getting out of my car, and I got hit by a truck."

I stared at him.

"So I wasn't looking," he said testily. "Shit happens."

"A pickup truck with oversized tires?"

His eyes narrowed.

I sat back down. "Tell me about it."

Lucero had been looking for Jeremy Stone for about a week, mostly hanging out in the bar he'd told me about. One afternoon, he parked his car at the curb near the bar, the way he usually did, and stepped out. A pickup truck was bearing down on him. He threw himself over the hood of his car, trying to get out of the way. The truck sideswiped his car, smashing his legs between the fenders of the two vehicles.

"I was lucky I wasn't killed."

"Any witnesses?"

"A few people on the street, but no one got the license number. I figured it was a goddamn drunk. And how did you know it was a pickup on big tires?"

I described the similar "accident" I'd had outside a bar a few days ago. Now it was his turn to stare, listening with his mouth open. Then he closed it, and his face set like cement.

"Son of a bitch," he said tightly.

"Exactly."

"It was Jeremy Stone."

"Or people connected with him. They had another try at me last night." I told him about my experience at the golf course. "I'd thought it had to do with Clare's death, her murderer making sure I didn't stumble onto anything. But there must be more to it than that."

"Got to be," Lucero said. "When that motherfucker tried to kill me, Clare Butler was still alive."

I nodded. "I need to find Stone."

"He's touchy about that."

"Right."

"If and when you find him, bring him up here and we'll dangle him over the balcony, see if he talks."

"There's a thought." I stood.

"Let me know what you find out, okay?"

"Sure."

"I wish I could go with you."

"Me, too."

I meant it. I had a feeling the closer I got to Stone, the more I'd need someone to watch my back. Especially since there was obviously an inside informant, someone who'd told Stone about me from the beginning.

That "someone" had to come from a short list, those who'd known I'd been hired: Oliver Westfall, Samuel Butler, and those close to Butler.

His children.

CHAPTER

20

BEFORE I LEFT GIL LUCERO'S APARTMENT, I phoned
Kenneth Butler and asked if I could come over.

"Now?" he said, put off. "It's after nine o'clock."

"It's important."

"Can't we do this over the phone?"

"I want to talk to Doreen, too." She was the one who'd
mentioned Jeremy Stone to the salesclerk.

"What about?" he asked sharply.

"Kenneth, this is all related to your father's defense.
Do you want to help me or not?" I could've mentioned
Jeremy Stone. But I wanted to see his face when I did.

"Yes, yes, all right. Do you know how to get here?"

"No."

He gave me directions.

The Butler residence was on Easter Avenue in Littleton,
the southeastern portion of the greater metro suburban
sprawl. Twenty years ago this area had been gently rolling
fields of scrub brush populated by prairie dogs and jackrabbits, with just enough coyotes and hawks hanging
around to keep their numbers in check. Now there were
curving streets and single-family dwellings, with nothing
to check the population—except perhaps the economy.

Which, come to think of it, was more brutal than hawks and coyotes.

The house was a wide, white, two-story frame fronted by a generous lawn, blue green in the light of the streetlamp. Square columns flanked the porch. One featured a sleeve for a flag pole. Over the front door was a brass eagle in bas-relief, wings spread, talons at the ready. Ready for what, I don't know. The prairie dogs and jackrabbits were long gone.

Kenneth must've been watching for me, because he opened the door before I got my thumb on the bell.

He greeted me with "I don't know why we couldn't do this over the phone."

"The telephone is so impersonal, don't you think?"

He blew air through his nostrils and led me into the living room. The furniture was colonial, more for show than comfort. Kenneth waved me to a chair, and I sat. He took the couch across from me. On the wall behind him, horsemen in red coats chased a bunch of beagles. The fox was safely out of the picture.

"All right, so what's this all about?"

"Where's your wife?"

He gave me the famous Butler scowl, as if my asking had somehow offended her honor. "Upstairs," he said, "putting the children to bed."

"I'd like to wait for her."

"I don't see any reason—"

He stopped when he heard her coming down the stairs. We waited expectantly, but it was a minute before she entered the room, clutching a pack of Virginia Slims and a thin silver lighter in her left hand. Apparently, she'd made a detour to fetch her smokes.

I stood, and Kenneth introduced us.

"It's a pleasure to meet you, Mr. Lomax," she said, smiling faintly.

"Likewise, I'm sure."

She was an extremely thin woman with pale red hair, fair skin, and large green eyes. Her eyes seemed even larger, set over drawn, almost gaunt cheeks. I could smell cigarette smoke on her clothes.

"Let's get this over with," Kenneth said impatiently.

Doreen sat beside him on the couch. I was struck by how dressed up they were. He wore a silk tie and a long-sleeved shirt, buttoned at the cuffs. Her dress was too fashionable for simply lounging around the house. Maybe they'd gone out to dinner. Or who knows? Maybe they'd dressed up for me.

"I appreciate your taking the time to see me," I said.

"Anything we can do to help Samuel," Doreen said. She fired up a cigarette and pulled a large ashtray close to her on the cherry-wood coffee table. Kenneth scowled. Dammit, Doreen, that ashtray is for decoration, not ashes.

"As you both know," I said, "or at least Kenneth does, Samuel believed Clare was having an affair and that her secret lover might've killed her."

"Yes, yes," Kenneth said. "So?"

"So, I may have found him."

Kenneth's thick eyebrows rose with effort from their resting place. "Really?"

"Who is he?" Doreen asked with interest.

"Actually, I haven't found the man, just his name."

They waited eagerly.

"Jeremy Stone," I said.

"Jer—" Doreen's jaw dropped, and she glanced fearfully at her husband. He looked at me as if I'd just set the carpet on fire. Jesus, not *too* obvious.

"Who . . . who is he?" Kenneth asked, straining to act nonchalant.

"I was hoping you could tell me."

138

"We don't know anyone by that name. Do we, Doreen."

He'd said it flatly, as if it were a statement, not a question. Doreen shook her head no and puffed on her cigarette.

I asked her, "Are you certain you don't know him?"

She blew out smoke and opened her mouth to speak.

"Of course she's certain," Kenneth said.

"Because Samuel Butler's freedom may depend on it," I said to Doreen. They stared back at me, Doreen frightened, Kenneth angry. I was getting a little angry myself.

"Not long before Clare Butler was murdered," I said, "she hired a private detective, Gil Lucero, to find Stone. Lucero talked to a salesclerk at a boutique in Cherry Creek. Doreen, the clerk said you'd been spending a lot of money in there lately and that you'd said it was all thanks to Jeremy Stone."

Kenneth shot Doreen an angry glance, then told me, "The clerk was mistaken."

"I wonder."

"Are you calling me a liar?" he said loudly.

"Perish the thought." I asked Doreen, "Was the clerk mistaken?"

". . . yes," she said in a small voice.

I think if she and I had been alone, I could've gotten her to talk to me. But she was too intimidated by her husband's presence. I tried to shake them up.

"Did you know that someone ran Lucero down with a truck."

"That doesn't mean—"

I cut off Kenneth: "He's still on crutches."

"What are you—"

"And last night someone tried to kill me."

"I . . ." Kenneth decided to say no more. Doreen's mouth was a tiny "o."

I let them feel the silence before I spoke. "It's obvious to me that Stone is involved in both of these murder attempts. And he may have killed Clare."

"No," Kenneth said. Doreen's expression had gone from apprehension to fright to horror. She directed it at Kenneth. He said, "I can assure you that . . ." He let his voice trail off.

"You can assure me what?"

He pressed his lips together and shook his head. "Nothing."

I wanted to yank him to his feet and slap him until he talked. Instead, I said, "Look, if you're afraid of Stone, maybe I can help."

Kenneth looked away. Doreen stared down at her ciga-rette. There wasn't much left but the filter. She stubbed it out in the sculptured ashtray.

"You're both pathetic," I said, standing. "You'd protect Stone and let Samuel go to prison for Clare's murder."

"My father is guilty," Kenneth said softly.

"You'd like to see him convicted, wouldn't you? That would leave you in charge of Butler Manufacturing."

His face had gone dark red, and I could tell he was ready to explode. I expected him to jump to his feet and start shouting, maybe even take a swing at me. I'd like that. But he just sat there, holding it in, hands together, fingers interlocked, squeezing the blood from his knuckles.

I shook my head at them and walked out. I would've slammed the door, but the kids were upstairs in bed.

I finished off the night in a neighborhood bar, swapping lies with the bartender and a couple of regulars, throwing down whiskey, and trying to get the Butlers out of my mind, the whole goddamn family.

I couldn't. There were things going on just out of my sight, and the Butlers were blocking my view. Obviously,

Kenneth and Doreen knew more than they were telling. But I had a feeling that Karen did, too. And Nicole and Wes. Hell, probably even Samuel. They gave out information reluctantly, as if they were all guarding some great secret.

Or maybe they were just like everyone else, trying to keep their personal lives private.

I left the bar when it closed.

As I stood in the lamp-lit street, fumbling with my car keys, I realized what an easy target I was. Killers roamed the land, and at least two of them were after me.

Let them come, I thought. I'm ready for them.

But I wasn't ready. I was just drunk.

I drove home with one bloodshot eye on the rearview mirror.

CHAPTER

21

I AWOKE FRIDAY MORNING with a mild hangover. A shower and a ham-and-egg breakfast helped. I poured another cup of coffee and phoned Oliver Westfall.

"I got your message yesterday." It seemed like days ago. "You said we have a problem."

"In a word," he said, "Winks. That is, Mr. Armbruster. He failed to appear Wednesday afternoon for his deposition."

"What about the other two, the flower vendor and the bartender?"

"Yes, they both came in, but their statements are nearly worthless. Mr. Colodny remembers the hundred-dollar bill he was given for the flowers but not exactly who gave it to him—other than the man in the photo you showed him."

"I was afraid of that."

"Yes, and although Mr. Stilwell recalls serving drinks to Mr. Butler, he can't positively state how Mr. Butler behaved or when he left the bar."

"Swell."

"The only man who can help us is Armbruster."

"I take it you've called him."

"He won't answer his phone. I'd like you to drive up there and convince him to come in."

"Okay." I only hoped Winks didn't mistake the smoky Toyota for an alien landing craft.

"I have more bad news," Westfall said. "I spoke to my contacts in Kansas City about Clare Butler's ex-pimp Sonny Washington. He may have wanted to kill Mrs. Butler, but he couldn't have done it. He had a meeting with his parole officer in Kansas City the day she was murdered. I'm afraid that eradicates my 'other suspect' defense."

"Oh, there are other suspects. In fact, three of them tried to kill me night before last."

"*What?*"

I described Wednesday night's golf outing and the shooting death of William Royce. I also told him the same truck that had run down Gil Lucero had barely missed me.

"Have you been to the police?"

"Absolutely. They even let me spend the night in their jail."

He ignored that and asked, "Who exactly did you speak with?"

"Lieutenant MacArthur."

"Does he believe these attempts on your life are connected with the Butler case?"

"I don't think he wants to. It might muss up his tidy murder case. But I may have found a connection—Jeremy Stone."

"Who's he?"

"Clare hired Lucero to find Stone about a week before he was run over. I don't know who Stone is or how he's involved. Maybe he killed Clare. If he did, then he might very well kill again to make sure Samuel Butler is convicted."

"Then our witnesses could be in danger."

"Probably just Winks," I said. "He's the only one who counts. Have you told anyone that I found him?"

"Samuel Butler. And my legal aide and my secretary, both of whom I trust implicitly. I'm certain neither of them have told anyone about Mr. Armbruster."

"Let's keep it that way."

"Yes, of course."

"I'll drive up and talk to Winks right away."

"Good. I'll be in the office all day, so bring him in if you can. Without coercing him, you understand."

"Perfectly."

"Oh, and I asked Mr. Butler what he knew of his wife's friend Madeline Tate. There was very little he could tell me, not even where she lives."

"That's all right. I found her."

We rang off.

I went outside into a fine spring day, with a sky so blue it made you smile. A couple of fat robins with red waistcoats and perfect posture hopped about Mrs. Finch's lawn, hunting for breakfast. One of them pecked the ground, snagged a night crawler, and began tugging it from the earth. The bird pulled, and the worm stretched, hanging on. It looked comical. Not to the worm, of course.

Which reminded me, there were two guys out there who'd like to stretch me out cold.

I kept one eye on the rearview mirror and drove off in the smoky Toyota. I gassed up at a service station on Broadway. Even remembered to check the oil. It was only down two and a half quarts. Then I headed west, still checking the mirror. No one seemed to be following.

On the way to Golden I thought about Madeline Tate.

Westfall's mention of her had reminded me of our conversation last night. My morbid emotional baggage. And how it was affecting my life.

Before Mexico, I'd been involved with a woman, Rachel Wynn. She'd been obliquely connected to a case I was working on, finding a runaway girl. We'd gone out a few times, dinner, a play. To bed. She was loving, sensitive, and beautiful. It would've been easy to fall in love with her. If I'd let myself. But I'd broken off the relationship and left town, gone south. Vacation. Right. I'd run away.

Because of Katherine.

I'd tried to tell myself that lots of guys lose their wives. One way or another. Some wives even die. A few are murdered.

But not murdered like that. Not tortured and sodomized and slashed and then thrown in a ditch like garbage. Not when her husband is an officer of the law, sworn to serve and protect. It had been my job, my *duty*. And I couldn't even save my own wife, my Katherine.

I'd never go through something like that again.

I *wouldn't*.

The monkey trap, Lomax. Goddammit, *let it go*.

The mountains had taken some snow last night, and the higher peaks were creamy white.

I skirted Golden on U.S. 6 and the bypass, then retraced the route Elliot had showed me last Monday—the snaky asphalt of Golden Gate Canyon Road, the ill-maintained dirt road, and finally the rocky path that led to Winks's home.

The house looked the same as it had last Monday, a hodgepodge of wings under continual construction. But something was different. It was quiet. There were no munchkin-sized monsters charging across the meadow to greet me. Maybe Winks had left and taken his dogs with him. If so, I'd make myself at home and wait for them all to return.

As I steered around the meadow, the Toyota disturbed a squawking of crows. They lifted from the tall grass on heavy wings, then settled back down as I passed, feasting on something.

I parked beside the house and shut off the engine. The house was quiet.

145

There was a battered pickup parked in the dirt near the door, so maybe Winks was home, after all. Unless he had two trucks.

I got out of the car and called his name.

The only answer was the faint screech of a hawk, adrift somewhere in the sea of sky. It gave me a chill. Or maybe it was just the cold mountain air.

I knocked on the screen door and called again. Silence. I pulled open the screen and tried the knob. Unlocked. Not too surprising, since a lot of mountain people leave their doors unlocked—few prowlers up here.

I pushed the door open and called Winks's name again. Nothing. Except for a bad odor, like rotting food. Then I saw something on the kitchen floor. It looked like an old, wadded-up rug. When I approached it, the flies rose, like tiny crows, and I saw that they'd been busy on one of Winks's dogs.

I unholstered the Magnum. Although I had the feeling that I was the only one here. Still, better safe than stupid.

I stepped around the carcass toward the doorway. The refrigerator kicked on, and I nearly put a bullet in it. Okay, so I was a *little* tense. I stood in the doorway and scanned the living room—a dirty hardwood floor, some heavy wooden chairs, an ancient couch draped with an Indian blanket, a stone fireplace with a flintlock rifle above the mantelpiece. A boot.

The scruffy brown boot stuck out from the other side of the couch, toe pointed at the ceiling.

I entered the room. The rotting smell was stronger in here. I moved around the couch.

The boot was on Winks's right foot. He lay between the couch and the fireplace, faceup in a halo of dried blood. Half a face up. The other half had been blown off, apparently by the shotgun that rested on the floor beside him.

Samuel Butler had told me that when he'd found

Clare's body, he could see her brain. Well, I could've seen Winks's brain except for all the flies in there. They buzzed angrily when I covered him with the blanket from the couch.

I put away the Magnum and looked around the room for signs of a struggle. There were no broken lamps or toppled furniture or bloody scuff marks on the dusty floor. Just Winks. An apparent suicide. At least it had been made to look that way.

I was no coroner, but even I could tell he'd been dead for more than a day, perhaps as many as three. Westfall had talked to him Tuesday afternoon, and Winks had failed to show up at his office Wednesday afternoon, so it had probably happened Tuesday night or Wednesday morning. Elementary.

On the other hand, Winks may have failed to show at Westfall's office for an entirely different reason, become despondent, killed his dogs—one in the kitchen and two in the meadow, for the crows—and then killed himself.

No way.

I felt certain he'd been murdered, probably by the same three shooters who'd tried to kill me Wednesday night. They'd probably come in politely, gaining his confidence, the way I had. Then they'd knocked him out, put the shotgun barrel under his jaw, and pulled the trigger. After that, they'd killed the dogs. Or maybe they'd killed the dogs first, while Winks was away, and then waited for him.

However it had happened, Winks was a blameless victim. He'd died because he'd shared drinks in a bar with Samuel Butler. And because I'd found him.

I could feel the guilt rising. I tried to quell it, tried to tell myself that his death wasn't my fault. And logically, it wasn't. I'd just been doing my job, trying to help Samuel Butler.

But my insides disagreed. I'd located Winks and thus

fingered him for the killers. They'd made me their accomplice—Jeremy Stone or his henchmen, whoever had done this.

I phoned the sheriff's department.

I took a last look at Winks's blanket-draped body, then went outside into the brittle sunshine.

CHAPTER

22

TWO SHERIFF'S DEPUTIES ARRIVED in a four-wheel-drive wagon with gold stars on the doors and a red, white, and blue light bar on the roof, turned off. They were big men with khaki uniforms and brown leather holsters. Their revolvers were still in the holsters, but they'd unsnapped the safety straps.

"I'm the man who called. Jacob Lomax." I had my ID out to prove it. "Mr. Armbruster's body is in the living room."

The older of the two, who was still younger than I, went in to see for himself. The other one took my ID and looked me over with soft brown eyes. They were the only things soft about him. He pointed at the bulge in my coat.

"Do you have a permit to carry a handgun, Mr. Lomax?"

"Yes, sir." I showed it to him.

The older deputy came outside, still breathing through his mouth. He sucked in a lungful of fresh air.

"Looks like a shotgun to the head," he said to his pal, "possibly self-inflicted." Then he turned to me. "Did you cover him with the blanket?"

"Yes, sir."

"Why?"

And so began the questioning, which passed the time as we waited for an inspector and the crime-scene technicians. The inspector had half a hundred questions of his own, and by the time they'd let me go and I'd driven back to Denver, it was nearly two in the afternoon.

I phoned Westfall from my office and gave him the bad news.

"Winks dead?" He didn't want to believe it.

"An apparent suicide."

"This is disastrous. We needed Winks's testimony. Without it I don't— What do you mean, 'apparent'?"

"I think he was murdered."

Westfall was silent for a moment. "What do the police think?"

"Probably suicide, unless they find evidence to the contrary. Winks was a bit off center. No one would be surprised if he killed himself. But you and I know there are people involved in this who are prepared to kill. And it was a little too convenient, Winks dying just before he was to testify on tape. Plus, there were the dogs."

"The what?"

"Winks's three dogs were killed, too. Maybe a suicide would take his pets with him, but I don't think Winks would do it like that—two in the meadow and one in the kitchen. Too disrespectful. Those animals were his closest companions."

"Did you tell this to the police?"

"No. It's only speculation."

"But you believe it was murder."

"I do."

"Then Mr. Colodny and Mr. Stilwell may be in danger."

"That depends," I said.

"On what?"

"On what you said to your people and Butler. Did

you tell them that Winks was the only witness that mattered?"

"I suppose I did," Westfall said. Then, "Wait a minute. Are you implying that one of them gave that information to the killers?"

"Do you have another explanation?"

Westfall was silent for what seemed a long time. Finally, he said, "I've known my people for too long to believe they'd be involved in anything like that."

"Perhaps one of them let it slip inadvertently. Maybe somebody asked them what seemed to be an innocent question."

"I'll speak to them."

"Let me know what you find out. In the meantime, I'll talk to Butler."

An hour later, I was in the county jail, facing Samuel Butler across the smudged tabletop in our enclosed booth.

He'd aged since I'd seen him four days ago, probably from lack of sleep. His face was pale, and there were bruised bags under his eyes. Even his green jumpsuit looked looser, as if he were shrinking inside it. He'd retained his scowl, but now it looked more the product of pain than anger. He slouched in his chair, shoulders hunched, eyes furtive, like a wildebeest in a cage.

"Winks is dead," I said.

"Winks?" He looked at me dully.

"Someone murdered him and made it look like suicide. Someone who wants you convicted."

"Killed Winks?"

Butler's mind was mushy. He wasn't used to being alone, nor could he handle being a ward. All his life he'd been in charge of everything—his business, his wife, his children. His second wife had been a struggle, but at least he'd *felt* in control. Now there were people who told him when to shower and sleep, when and what to eat, what to wear, who he could see. Other people would decide his fate. He was powerless. It was driving him inside himself, probably to a place he'd rarely seen.

"They killed Winks," I said, "because he was your best witness. Who did you tell about him?"

"What?"

I tried not to grind my teeth. "Who have you seen besides Westfall?"

"I don't remember."

I could probably get a look at the visitor's log, but I said, "Come on, Butler, snap out of it."

"What do you mean?"

"Wake the fuck up!"

Color rose to his cheeks. "You don't talk to me like that, you son of a bitch."

Good. "What visitors have you had in the past few days besides me and Westfall?"

He glared at me, but at least he was awake now. "Who do you think?" he snapped. "My children."

"Anyone else?"

"No."

"Did you tell them about Winks?"

"I don't know. Probably. What difference does it make?" He was sitting up straight now, face flushed, fire in his eyes. On him it looked healthy.

"Somebody told the killer about Winks—either one of your kids or one of Westfall's people. Inadvertently or on purpose."

"If it was from Kenneth or Karen or Nicole, it was inadvertently."

"Did you tell each of them?"

"I said so, didn't I?" He forced air through his nose. "They visit me every day, and there's not that much to talk about."

"Did you talk about Jeremy Stone?"

152

"Who?"

"You don't know him?"

"No."

"Could he be involved with Butler Manufacturing without your knowledge?"

Butler's scowl deepened. "What are you getting at?"

"Just answer the question."

His face turned a shade darker. He wished we were in his office so he could throw me out. Or maybe punch me out. Finally, he said, "It's possible."

"So Jeremy Stone could be employed by Butler Manufacturing or be a customer or a supplier and you wouldn't know about it?"

"In case you haven't noticed, I've been away from things for a few weeks."

"What about before that? Could he have been involved with your company before you were arrested?"

Butler shrugged his heavy shoulders. "I suppose. Sure."

"I thought you ran the business."

"I *do* run it!" He came out of his chair, ready to rip off the tabletop and beat me with it. At that moment it wasn't too hard to picture him standing behind Clare in their kitchen, a wrench in his fist. Now he glanced furtively at the window in the door. The guard was outside, looking in. Butler sat down.

"I do run it," he said with controlled fury. "Through Kenneth. And I'll be running it again firsthand, just like the old days, as soon as I get out."

If you get out. I said, "By 'the old days,' you mean before jail."

He shook his head and looked down at his hands. "Before Clare."

The rage had gone out of him, and his color had returned to jailhouse pale. His thoughts were in the past. I gave him a few moments before I asked, "What was it like before Clare?"

153

One corner of his mouth went up, and he shook his head again. "Simpler," he said, still not looking at me. Now his eyes rose to mine. "Everything was simpler before her." He laughed once, without mirth. "But, hey, who needs simple?"

"What about the business. What was simple about it before Clare?"

"The business was the same. I was different. More focused."

I waited.

He sighed. "I built Butler Manufacturing from scratch, starting in my garage. When the business grew beyond what I could handle myself, I had a hard time hiring anyone. Not that there weren't plenty of available people. But I wanted to find someone who'd *love* the business. Wrong. All I needed was someone to glue on emblems for an hourly wage. Once I figured that out, hell, I didn't care if they *hated* the job as long as the finished product was up to my standards."

A prince of a man to work for. "But you knew the names of all your employees."

"Hell yes. At first. The business kept growing, though. When Kenneth graduated from C.U., I brought him in as my assistant. He had a bachelor's degree in accounting, so naturally I let him do the books. And as we needed more people, I let him do the hiring, too."

"What did you do?"

"I dealt with customers and sales reps and kept an eye on production. I spent half the day in the back, making sure things were done right, were made right, before they got shipped out. *That's* the key to a business. Your end product."

"How could you be around those people four hours a day and not know their names?"

"I knew their names. Some of them. First names, anyway. Hell, I've got thirty or forty employees. How am I supposed to know them all? They call me Mr. Butler, and

154

I call them Hey You. What difference does it make? As long as the books show a profit."

A model businessman. "So at least you looked at the books."

"Damn right I looked at them. The bottom line, anyway."

"How about after you met Clare?"

"Well, like I said, that's when things changed. Clare was a distraction." He actually grinned. A first, as far as I knew. It made him look stupid. "I started spending most of my time with her and very little time at work." His grin widened. "For the first time in my life I had fun. We . . . played. Trips and shopping sprees and the rest of it."

"While you were playing, did Kenneth look after the business?"

He nodded. "Naturally, I'd check in now and then, make sure everything was running smoothly."

"Check the bottom line."

"That's it."

"And if—I mean, when you get out, you'll assume command of the company."

"Right."

"Take it away from Kenneth."

"Well . . . he'll still be my number-one assistant. He knows that."

"I'm sure he does."

"Hey, he's my son. He knows what's what. He'll take over everything when I retire."

Or when you go to prison. I said, "I'd like a look at the company's books."

"What for?"

"To see if Jeremy Stone is an employee or a customer or whatever."

"Why don't you just ask Kenneth about Stone?"

"I already did. He says he's never heard of him. That's why I want to see the books."

Some of the color returned to his face. "Are you calling my son a liar?"

"I just want to cover every base."

"If he wants to show you the books, that's his decision. He's in charge now. But I'm sure he's got nothing to hide."

I nearly said, Don't bet your life on it. But he probably was. I said, "One more question. About Clare."

"What?"

"Had she been doing drugs?"

"Hell no."

"You're sure?"

"Hey, she was my wife."

Right. Clare was his wife, Kenneth was his son, and Butler Manufacturing was his company—and he didn't know squat about any of them.

CHAPTER

23

AFTER I LEFT SAMUEL BUTLER in the county jail, I drove
to my office and phoned Oliver Westfall. He told me that
both his secretary and his legal aide swore they'd told
no one about Russ "Winks" Armbruster, nor had anyone
asked.

"Butler told Kenneth, Karen, and Nicole," I said.

"My God, you're not suggesting that one of *them* had
anything to do with Winks's death."

"It's possible one of them, or maybe Wes Hartman or
Doreen, passed on the information, perhaps innocently.
In any event, I want to go through the books of Butler
Manufacturing—payroll, accounts payable, and so on."

"Why?"

"To try to find some reference to Jeremy Stone."

"I'm sure Kenneth Butler will allow you—"

"I'm sure he won't. Can you force him to show me?"

"On what grounds?"

"That it's crucial to his father's defense."

Westfall hesitated. "Is it crucial?"

"I don't know."

"Do you have any material evidence to present to a
judge?"

"No."

"In that case, no one can force him to open his books. Except the IRS, of course."

After we hung up, I turned to the phone book and found a pageful of Stones. No Jeremy. Plenty of J's, though. I checked my watch—a bit after three. I'd have better luck calling these folks later, when they were all home from work.

But as secretive as my Jeremy Stone seemed to be, he probably had an unlisted number. Of course, if he lived in Colorado, he almost certainly had a Colorado driver's license. And that's public information.

I drove to the motor vehicle bureau on West Mississippi Avenue. It took me two or three clerks, but eventually I got Xerox copies of Jeremy Stone's driver's license. *Licenses*. There were three, each with a different middle name, description, and address.

Jeremy Holcroft Stone was fifty-three, wore glasses, and lived in upscale Cherry Hills. Jeremy Thomas Stone, sixty-nine, of working-class Arvada, also wore glasses; his hair and mustache were gray. Jeremy Leonard Stone was twenty-six, lived in economically depressed west Denver, and had a scar over his left eye.

I'd gone from zero Stones to three. Which was mine? Perhaps none of them. And I was dead certain if I asked each of them if they knew Kenneth or Doreen Butler, I'd get three negative replies.

I needed some definite way to identify *the* Jeremy Stone. I needed a look at Butler's books.

I drove to Butler Manufacturing Company and found a place for the Toyota in the crowded front lot. Inside, the four women were still at their desks—two typing, two on the phone. Between phone calls I told one of them I wanted to see Kenneth Butler.

"He's with a customer in his office. You'll have to wait."

"No problem," I said, but she was already talking on

the phone, wheedling money from a slow-paying customer.

I wandered into the hallway. It ended at a door marked Employees Only. I glanced into the office. All four women were hard at work, and I sure didn't want to disturb them by asking permission, so I walked down the hall and pushed through the door.

The production area of Butler Manufacturing was a maze of long worktables and eight-foot-high shelves spread beneath a steel-girder roof. Fluorescent light fixtures dangled overhead from long, thin wires. From where I stood, I could see a few dozen workers—men and women, young and old. Some were pushing handcarts or stocking or emptying shelves. But most were busy at their worktables. A few people glanced my way, but no one ran over to throw me out, so I began strolling about.

There was a quiet murmur of conversation and an occasional laugh. I noticed more than one person wearing headphones, plugged into their private sounds.

At a nearby table I watched three people armed with hand-held propane burners soldering tiny nails to the backs of little cloisonné American flags. Lapel pins, I guessed, thousands of them. Farther along I saw the logos for baseball teams being Super Glued to ballpoint pens. And truck emblems being attached to belt buckles. And a computer company's logo being glued to key holders. And . . .

"Can I help you?"

She had long brown hair tied in a ponytail. Late teens, T-shirt and jeans. Her smile was genuine, but she had a sad face, with large, wet brown eyes. She'd been pushing a rubber-wheeled cart laden with small boxes.

"Yes, I'm looking for Jeremy Stone."

Her delicate brows went up, making her eyes even larger.

"Does he work here?"

"I believe he does."

MICHAEL ALLEGRETTO

She shook her head. "There's *Jerry* who works in shipping, but I don't know his last name. We could ask."

I followed her down a long, wide aisle formed by free-standing metal shelves. At the rear of the building was a loading bay, its wide steel door rolled up. A couple of guys were carrying boxes into the rear of a semitrailer. The driver, a wiry little man with a thin mustache, looked on, arms folded. Loading was not in his job description.

"What about those?" he asked one of the guys, and nodded toward boxes stacked beside the door.

"Some are for UPS, and some go out tomorrow."

The brown-eyed girl rolled her cart past the men to a long table against the rear wall. The young guy working there was hefty, with short blond hair and acne scars on the back of his neck. A cigarette was tucked behind one ear. He wore jeans, running shoes, and a T-shirt, which seemed to be the uniform of the day at Butler Manufacturing. He wrapped packing tape around a box, slapped on a shipping label, and made a notation on a clipboard.

"Jerry?"

He turned around, glanced at me, then frowned at the cart.

"Geez, Molly, these aren't going out today, are they? It's almost quitting time."

"I don't think so." She pulled an order form from between two boxes and handed it to Jerry.

He scanned the sheet, then said, "Northfield Distributing, Minneapolis. More of these cheap plastic mugs. They go tomorrow. Would you put them over there?"

"Sure, ah, Jerry? This man wants to ask you something."

"Yeah?"

"I'm looking for Jeremy Stone," I told him.

His eyebrows went together briefly, then straightened out. "Don't know him."

"He's supposed to work here," Molly put in.

160

Jerry shook his head. "There's no one here by that name."

"You're sure?"

"Yeah, I'm sure. I've worked here for five years, and I've never heard of the guy."

"Could Jeremy Stone be a customer? Or a supplier?"

His brows pushed together, and he shook his head slowly. "I've never seen that name on an invoice. Of course, he might own a company with a name other than—"

"What are you doing back here?"

We all turned to see Kenneth Butler hustling toward us—jacket off, sleeves rolled up, tie unloosened. He looked ready to fight. Molly got busy unloading her cart, and Jerry turned to his table.

"Hi, Kenneth."

"Didn't you see the sign?" he asked angrily.

I shrugged. "So who's smoking?"

"Employees Only," he snapped.

"I must've missed that one."

"I want you out of here. Now."

"Good," I said, motioning for him to lead the way. "We can talk in private."

Molly was watching us out of the corner of her eye. I winked at her, and she looked away. Then I quickly scanned the rear of the building. In addition to the loading-bay door, there was an exit door, closed, with telltale wires running along the top frame. There were also small hinged windows near the ceiling. As I turned to go after Kenneth, an employee pushed one closed with a long pole.

Kenneth led me through the Employees Only door, up the hallway, and past the outer office. He pointed to the front entrance. I saw wires over the top frame. Beside the doorframe was a metal box with a keyhole and a pair of LEDs, one red, one green. The green one was lit.

161

"Out," he recommended.

It seemed presumptuous to ask him for a look at his books.

"We'll talk again," I told him.

I drove off in the smoky Toyota and headed for Home Club to buy a ladder.

CHAPTER

24

IT WAS MIDNIGHT WHEN I RETURNED to Butler Manufacturing.

I steered the Toyota down a gentle incline and around to the rear of the building. The loading area was well lighted but mostly hidden from the street. Of course, if a cop, real or rent-a, checked back here, it would prove embarrassing. Honest, Officer, I was only washing windows.

I climbed out and zipped up my jacket against the chill air. Then I untied the cords from the front and rear bumpers and dragged the extension ladder from the roof of the car. It was aluminum, light but still awkward to handle. I carried it to the rear of the building and ran up the extension. It rattled loudly, the sound echoing off the cinder-block wall and asphalt yard.

I waited, listening for sirens. Nothing. I heard a car go by on Dartmouth.

I leaned the ladder against the building and positioned it under a small, high window near the loading dock. The window was about fifteen feet up, and the ladder didn't quite reach it. I belted on my tool pouch and climbed the ladder. Slowly, because it wobbled.

The window was covered by a heavy mesh screen, fastened at the corners with hex-head bolts. I took out three

MICHAEL ALLEGRETTO

of the bolts with a snap-on ratchet wrench and dropped them in my pouch, then pivoted the screen on the remaining bolt, letting it hang beneath the metal-cased window.

This afternoon, when I'd been inside, I'd seen wires for the burglar alarm on all the doors, but not on the upper windows. Still, it was nerve-racking to force the window lock with a heavy screwdriver and wait for the clang of alarm bells.

Silence.

I pushed the window open. It was hinged on the bottom, and it swung in about forty-five degrees, stopped there by its chain. I unhooked the chain and eased the window all the way down until it lay flat against the inside wall.

Then I switched on my flashlight and shone it inside the cavernous building. I was above the fluorescent light fixtures, and they looked like long, pale coffins floating in air. The shelves and tables below were ominous dark shapes. I shone my light straight down. The concrete floor wasn't down quite as far as the asphalt outside—perhaps twelve feet.

I switched off the light, tucked it in my pouch, and climbed through the window opening feet first. Then I rolled over, and the windowsill bit into my stomach, my arms, my hands. I dangled for a moment over the abyss, then let go. It was only about a four-foot drop, but my ankles hurt when I landed. I'm too old for this shit.

I switched on the flashlight and made my way through the work area to the front, trying to ignore what I'd left outside: abandoned car, open window, ladder. A trifle suspicious.

Quickly, I walked up the hallway, then through the outer office to Kenneth's office. The door was closed and locked. I picked it open.

I went directly to the file cabinets and the personnel records. They were in alphabetical order, a file for each employee, containing name, address, phone number, names of spouses and children, original job application, health insurance information, and so on.

There was no file for Jeremy Stone.

I found the accounting books in a bottom drawer— money owed, due, received, paid. Company names only.

Next I pawed through invoices and shipping statements. Nothing. I scanned thick folders of business correspondence. No letters to or from Jeremy Stone.

Not a goddamn thing.

I shone my light on Kenneth Butler's desk. There was a telephone, a stack of catalogs, and a Rolodex. I flipped through all the S's. No Stone, Jeremy. I flipped through the J's. No Jeremy Stone.

End of the line. Christ, I'd thought I'd find *something*.

I started to leave. And then I remembered my first visit here last Monday. When I'd walked in, a ledger had been open on the desk. Kenneth had shoved it in the drawer. Nervously, it had seemed.

I stepped around to the business side of the desk, picked open the lock on the wide, shallow drawer, and slid it open. Inside was a big book with a green cover. I laid it open—the payroll record for Butler Manufacturing. The employees were listed in alphabetical order. And there he was, near the bottom of the page—Jeremy Stone. Name, social security number, salary, federal and state withholding, FICA, and net earnings. I turned pages and found Stone on every one. Since the first of the year he'd been clearing just under two thousand dollars every other week. Which meant he took home about fifty grand a year. Not bad for an employee who no one had ever heard of.

I scanned the column of net earnings. The employees'

salaries ranged from $12,000 to $24,000, with the exception of Kenneth Butler, who made a tidy $75,000. He was the only one who made more than Jeremy Stone, and Stone made twice as much as anybody else—including, I noticed, Wes Hartman.

What did Jeremy Stone do for his money?

I ran my finger up the column to Stone's social security number and carefully copied that most sacred nine-digit identifier, as personal and individual as a set of fingerprints. Then I locked the ledger in the desk drawer and left the office, pulling the door closed behind me. I moved through the outer office to the hallway.

A car pulled up out front.

For a moment I froze, unsure whether to duck back and hide in the office. If the people in the car (cops?) went back there, I'd be trapped. On the other hand, if I chose the hallway, there was a good chance I'd be seen through the glass front door before I made it to the Employees Only door. But the work area had a number of exits, including an open window.

I sprinted down the hall, shouldered through the door, and pushed it closed.

The outside lock clicked open, and there was sudden light under the door, shining on the toes of my shoes.

I hurried through the shadowy maze of tables and shelves to the rear of the building. Then the overhead lights flickered and came on, filling the area with cold white light. I hunkered down behind a rack of shelves and waited for someone to tell me to come out with my hands up.

No one did.

There were footsteps on the concrete. They moved past me. I peeked around the shelves.

Wes Hartman was walking away from me, carrying a gym bag in one hand.

What the hell was he doing here at midnight?

Maybe he'd driven by, seen my car and ladder, and come in to investigate. Although his movements weren't guarded or tense. He walked purposely, shoulders back, head erect.

He moved out of sight. I considered hustling out the front door. But someone else might be waiting there. Besides, I was curious about Hartman.

I crept after him, careful not to make a sound.

He walked directly to the packing area near the loading dock. A few dozen boxes were stacked there, ready to be shipped tomorrow, some the size of beer cases, some smaller. Hartman began unstacking boxes, checking labels. He found the one he was looking for and slit the packing tape with a pocket knife. He opened the box, then opened the gym bag beside it. His back was to me, blocking my view, but it looked as if he were taking something out of the box and putting it in his bag.

What was he doing, stealing belt buckles?

I considered stepping up and scaring the shit out of him, demanding to know what he was doing. Of course, he could demand the same of me. And no matter who called the cops, *I'd* be the one busted for breaking and entering.

I moved down the row of shelves, hoping for a look at what he was taking.

I bumped a table.

I froze, holding my breath. I hadn't made much of a sound. Perhaps Hartman hadn't heard.

"Who's there?" he said loudly.

Oh, fine.

"Is someone in here?"

I curled up under a table. I couldn't see Hartman. But I could hear him moving toward me. And then he was standing right beside me. From my vantage point all I could see were his fancy running shoes and faded designer jeans. I waited for him to look under the table. Hi, Wes, I dropped a contact. He stood there for a moment, then moved away. Only now could I see that he was carrying a gun.

He held it before him, pivoting this way and that. Then he returned to the rear of the building and the packing area. I opted to stay put.

After a few minutes, I heard him walking through the building to the front. Then the light went out.

I uncurled from my burrow, flipped on my flashlight, and made my way to the front. There was no light under the door. I heard the muffled sound of a car start and drive off.

I walked back to the packing table.

The stacks of boxes looked undisturbed. I began moving boxes around, trying to find the one that Hartman had cut open. But he'd either taken it with him or resealed it, because none of the boxes appeared to have been tampered with. Of course, even if I could identify the box, I probably couldn't tell what he'd removed.

I dragged a table under the open window. Apparently, Hartman had been too preoccupied to notice it. I climbed onto the table, jumped up, grabbed the windowsill, and pulled myself into the opening. It was awkward as hell to get myself turned around. I stood on the ladder, reached into the opening, and pulled the window up. I refastened the chain and pulled the window closed. Then I pivoted the wire screen over the window and replaced the corner bolts. What if the cops showed up now? Busted for fixing and leaving.

I tossed my tools in the trunk of the Toyota, tied the ladder to the roof, and drove away.

I wondered what Wes Hartman considered valuable enough to steal from Butler Manufacturing. And was it just a coincidence that I'd gone in there the same night as Hartman? Or was this something he did every night?

CHAPTER

25

ON SATURDAY MORNING, I presented George the handy-
man with an almost new ladder, used only once.

I'd found him on the south side of the house, plucking
tiny weeds from Mrs. Finch's tulip bed. He looked
shrunken inside his faded blue work shirt and Big Ben
overalls, the cuffs rolled twice to clear the square toes of
his old boots. His face was as brown and wrinkled as
yesterday's lunch sack. His hands were too big for his
body—knobby, gnarly, yellow-nailed things, tough as ju-
niper roots.

He squinted one eye at the ladder.

"What's wrong with it?" He had a voice like a cat claw-
ing sandpaper.

"Nothing."

"Why do you want to give it to me?"

"You can use it, can't you?"

"Sure. Can't you?"

"No, George, I can't." Take the damn thing.

"Where'd you get it?"

"I bo— I found it. Sort of."

"Oh?" Tell me more.

"I saw it fall off the back of a truck."

"Ah."

"I waved at the driver, but he didn't see me."

"Ah-ha."

"I thought about putting an ad in the paper, but who reads those things?"

He was still squinting, but not quite as hard. "Let me see it." He took the ladder from me and began inspecting it as if I were a traveling salesman.

"How much you want for it?"

"Nothing, George, it's yours."

"Hmm."

Je-*sus*. "On one condition."

"Oh?"

"You don't tell anybody you got it from me, you understand? You bought it. I never saw it before in my life."

"Gotcha," he said, and hauled it into the backyard, the proud new owner of a ladder with a past.

I put gas and oil in the Toyota and drove west.

The driver's licenses for two of the three Jeremy Stones included social security numbers, an option in Colorado. One of them matched the number I'd lifted from the payroll book of Butler Manufacturing.

Jeremy Leonard Stone. My man.

The copy of his license photo wasn't too sharp, but Stone was a mean-looking dude. Maybe it was the scar over his eye. Or maybe it was the possibility that he'd been involved in a murder or two, not to mention a couple of attempts on *my* life. Yeah, that would definitely ugly him up.

The address was in west Denver, just off the Sixth Avenue Freeway, a neighborhood of small, frame houses. Jeremy Stone's needed paint.

It was a dirty white cracker box with a patched roof, faded fake shutters, and yellow-stained rain gutters. The yard had yet to be mowed this year, and there were clumps of grass half a foot high, probably where the neighborhood dogs had dropped their fertilizer. Wind-

171

blown papers decorated the front stoop. The screen door hung open, its restraining spring broken and the wire mesh sagging with age.

Butler Manufacturing pays this guy fifty grand a year?

Maybe this wasn't my man, after all. But no, the numbers matched. It had to be him.

I unholstered the Magnum and held it behind my leg.

The doorbell button had been painted over years ago, so I banged a fist on the door.

It was opened by a corpulent woman in a green blouse and blue pants. Her round face was free of makeup and framed by limp blond hair. She had watery blue eyes, set too close together.

"What is it?" she demanded, frowning.

"Are you Mrs. Jeremy Stone?"

"Are you from the collection agency?"

"No."

"Then whatever you're selling, I ain't buying."

"I'm not selling anything." Jesus, her and George. "I'm looking for your husband."

She smirked. "What for?"

"It's a police matter."

She snorted through her pug nose. "You're just a little too late, mister."

"Excuse me?"

"He's dead."

"What?"

"That's right." She smiled at my obvious confusion.

"Since when?"

"A year ago last January."

"A year . . ."

"Look, mister, I got things need tending," she said, and shut the door in my face.

I put away the Magnum, held up a card, and knocked on the door. After a couple of pounding footsteps, it was yanked open.

172

"Now look here, I already told you—"

"Mrs. Stone, I'm a private investigator working on a murder case and—"

"Murder?" Her eyes got round.

"That's right. I need to ask you a few questions."

She blinked a few times, then glanced at my card and shook her head. "No. Jeremy had his faults, but he wasn't no *murderer*."

"I didn't say he was. Perhaps we should talk inside."

She hesitated, then let me into the stale-smelling living room. It was furnished in neo-American recession, with duct-tape patches on the carpet, pictures of Jesus and Elvis on the walls, and neglected plants on the end tables. Even the flowers on the wallpaper needed watering. Beside the sagging secondhand sofa was an ironing board and stacks of clothes—all arranged to face a color TV that had only two colors. A greenish John Wayne argued soundlessly with a purplish Maureen O'Hara. Mrs. Stone took the sofa. She left the TV on. I handed her the copy of Jeremy Leonard Stone's license, then sat in a lumpy armchair.

"Is that your husband?"

She held the paper with two fingers, scrunched up her mouth, and nodded slightly. "That's him, all right." Then she looked up at me. "Say, where'd you get this?"

"Official sources," I said, like a big shot. "Tell me, Mrs. Stone, where did your husband work?"

Her hand dropped to the sofa seat, the paper still pinched between thumb and forefinger. "Pittman Brothers. They're roofers."

"Is that what your husband did, reshingle roofs?"

She nodded. "When the son of a bitch worked. Mostly, he drank."

"How much did they pay him?"

"What do you care?"

173

"Personally, I don't. It's just police business," as if that meant something.

She shook her head and stared at the TV. I watched John sweep Maureen off her feet, carry her into the bedroom of their small Irish cottage, and dump her on the bed. The bed broke.

"He was lucky if he took home a thousand dollars a month."

"I see." According to Butler's books, Jeremy Stone earned that much in a week. "Did he ever work for a company called Butler Manufacturing?"

"I don't know, maybe before I met him."

"When was that?"

"We was married for three years."

"Mrs. Stone, I don't mean to be impolite, but may I ask how your husband died?"

"Car wreck," she said bitterly.

"What happened?"

"He was drunk, as usual, coming home from one of his bars. He drove off the street and ran smack into a tree. Broke his neck, the dumb son of a bitch. Left me with a stack of bills, and I can't find no more than part-time work. I have to take in ironing just to make ends meet. Times is tough, I don't give a damn what they say."

"Mrs. Stone, did your husband ever mention a man named Samuel Butler?"

"Butler?" She shook her head. "Nope."

"What about Kenneth Butler or Clare Butler?"

"I don't know no Butlers."

"How about Wes Hartman?"

"Him neither."

I tried one more shot, the shooter William Royce.

"Never heard of him," she said. "Now which one of them liars said Jeremy killed somebody?"

"None of them did."

174

"Okay, then." She waved her hand to show me the door.

I left.

She stayed on the couch, staring at Maureen, alone on the broken bed.

CHAPTER

26

I COULD THINK OF ONLY ONE REASON for Butler Manufacturing to have a dead man on their payroll. And since Clare Butler had been looking for that man, it was fairly clear why she'd been killed. And by whom.

But I wanted to clarify a few details before I took it to the police.

From a phone booth at a gas station I called Butler Manufacturing to see if they were open on Saturday. They were. I asked for Kenneth. The girl said Mr. Butler would be with me in a minute. I hung up and drove to Butler's house.

It wasn't Kenneth I wanted to question. It was Doreen. She might resist, but she'd be a hell of a lot more willing to talk than her husband.

I parked in the street before the wide white two-story house. The next-door neighbors were tending their yard. They looked with distaste and suspicion at my beat-up Toyota. Okay, so we're not all middle class.

I went up the walk and rang the bell. The brass eagle over the door was still alert, talons at the ready.

Doreen Butler opened the door wearing a purple sweat suit and a surprised look. She held a rag and a bottle of lemon oil in her right hand and the doorknob in her left.

"If you're looking for Kenneth, he's at work."

She wasn't about to let me in.

"It's you I want to talk with, Mrs. Butler."

"I—I have nothing to say to you, not until my husband gets home. Good-bye."

She started to close the door.

"If I leave here now, I go straight to the police."

Doreen hesitated. She seemed to be hiding behind the door like a frightened child. I could see only half of her gaunt white face and one large green eye.

"The police?" Her voice was small.

"I just had a chat with Mrs. Jeremy Leonard Stone."

Her green eye got a little wider, flitting from my face to the ground and back again.

"Her husband's been dead for more than a year," I said, not telling her anything she didn't already know. "And he's currently on the payroll of Butler Manufacturing."

She hesitated, then pulled the door open and walked away. I went inside and closed it behind me.

I found her in the living room, fumbling with a pack of cigarettes. She'd set the rag and lemon oil on the cherrywood coffee table. She managed to shake a butt loose from the pack, then fired it up with her silver lighter. Now she crossed her arms so tightly that she could barely raise her hand to suck in smoke. I'd seen tennis rackets strung with less tension.

"Perhaps you should sit down," I suggested.

She dropped immediately to the couch, knees together, elbows in, still the frightened child. I wanted cooperation, but this was ridiculous.

"Where are your children?"

"What? No, I won't allow them to hear this."

"Of course not. That's why I asked."

"Oh. They're . . . playing in the backyard."

I nodded.

"You know—" she blurted.

I waited.

"You know we didn't do anything wrong. Not really."

"Kenneth stole from the company, and you knew about it. That makes him a thief and you an accessory."

"But—"

"Not to mention forgery and filing phony tax information."

She sucked on her cigarette. An inch of ash jutted precariously from the end. She looked nervously around for someplace to drop it. There was a sculpted ashtray on the floor where she'd set it before wiping down the table. I placed it in front of her.

"Tell me how it started," I said.

She reached toward the ashtray, but the ash fell too soon, imploding dryly on the shiny cherry wood. Doreen wiped it hastily with her hand, leaving a grayish white smudge.

"It's all Samuel's fault," she said bitterly.

"How so?"

"He's never been fair with Kenneth. He's picked on him and criticized him his whole life. Never rewarded him. Never gave him what he'd earned, what he *deserved*."

Her voice had become shrill. She winced, aware of it. She put out her cigarette in the ashtray with quick, vicious little jabs and immediately lit another.

"A salary of seventy-five thousand a year seems fairly rewarding to me," I said.

"For running the entire company?" She blew smoke noisily. "Samuel does practically nothing, and he takes home a couple hundred thousand. At least he did when that whore was alive."

"Clare?"

"Who else? He spent money on her like there was no tomorrow."

"For her there wasn't."

The anger drained from her face, leaving it pale and gaunt. She looked away and sucked her cigarette.

"I don't know why I'm telling you any of this," she said quietly.

I waited for her to think of a reason.

Finally, she said, "You have to know how Samuel controlled things to understand."

"By 'things' you mean money."

She gave me a half grin that quickly died. "We're all officers in the corporation of Butler Manufacturing—Kenneth, me, Karen, Nicole, I think even Wes—but it's in name only. Samuel owns one hundred percent of the stock, and he distributes the profits as he sees fit. We each get a yearly 'bonus.' And listen to this: Karen and Nicole each get more than Kenneth and me put together. Now you tell me, is that fair?"

I said nothing.

"He always treated his daughters better than Kenneth," she continued. "He spoiled Nicole rotten, gave her anything she wanted. His little baby. Even kept her room for her after he married Clare. And Karen, he practically bought that shop for her. His princess." She snorted. "I doubt he even knows she's a lesb—"

"She's what?"

"It doesn't matter." She took a long drag, blew out a stream of smoke, and shook her head.

"You were telling me about the company profits."

She sighed. "Samuel gave us all bonuses, but there's still a lot left over. A *lot*. And you know what Samuel does with it? Socks it away, that's what. Puts it in stocks, bonds, trust funds, money markets, and so on."

"Trust funds for whom? Your children?"

"Hah! If only it were so. The beneficiaries are our *grand*children. Do you understand? The children of my children, who aren't even born yet and—who knows?—may never exist. And for *their* children. He's providing

179

for the children of people who may never be born. It's just insane." She savagely jammed her cigarette into the ashtray, pretending it was Samuel Butler's face. She picked up the pack, stared at it for a moment, then tossed it on the table as if she'd decided to break the habit. "And his will is the same way," she said. "I've seen a copy of it. We, the living, will get very little. The unborn get the rest."

She was silent for a moment, lost in her justifications.

"So you decided to correct that."

Another half grin. "Correct. That's exactly the right word. We got the idea from a newspaper story. Actually, I was the one who saw it," she said with some pride, and now she shook a cigarette loose from her pack and lit it. "A bookkeeper for a company in Pennsylvania created a phantom employee and cashed the extra paycheck himself. The IRS eventually caught him because the phantom employee never paid his income tax. Kenneth solved that problem by using a real name and matching social security number and paying withholding tax."

She blew smoke from her mouth and nostrils and continued, "At the library we looked through the obituaries in last year's newspapers and picked half a dozen names in low income neighborhoods. Kenneth phoned the families and gave them some story about being with a finance company and offering an easy line of credit. All they had to do was mail him a copy of their latest income tax form. A few did. Mrs. Stone's was a joint filing. She'd signed her husband's name, but made no indication that he'd died or that this was his final tax form—which was what Kenneth was looking for. As far as the IRS was concerned, Jeremy Stone was still alive.

"Kenneth opened a bank account in Stone's name with a post office box for his address. Next year he planned to file Stone's income tax forms. And if the company were audited, all the figures would check. The feds would be happy."

"Very thorough. But weren't you afraid Samuel might notice a sudden increase in his payroll?"

"No. Kenneth had been doing the books for years. The payroll, too. After Samuel met Clare, he hardly looked at the books. Oh, he kept an eye on *Kenneth's* salary. But the company was the farthest thing from his mind."

"If he went to prison, it'd be even farther."

"That was never our intention. It was—" She looked at me with a pleading expression. "It was an *accident*."

'What was an ac—"

I was interrupted by the back door banging open followed by high-pitched yelling and footsteps running through the kitchen. A boy and a girl burst into the living room, shouting for their mother.

"He pushed me down!"

"Did not!"

"Did so!"

"Because she threw dirt on me!"

"Did not!"

They were around seven or eight years old. The girl had her mother's pale red hair and green eyes and wore a sweater, plaid skirt, and knee socks. The boy had on blue jeans, a Colorado Rockies' jacket, and the famous Butler scowl. They barely noticed me, another piece of furniture.

"She started it!"

"He did!"

"All right," Doreen said tightly, "let's all calm down."

"But he pushed me!"

"Did not!"

"That's *enough!*" Doreen shouted.

The two kids stared at her with eyes wide and mouths open. They weren't accustomed to their mother raising her voice. Neither was she. Her hand shook. So did her voice.

"Now, please. Mother has company. Go outside and play."

They stared at her a moment longer, their expressions sullen. Then they turned and walked out, shoulder to shoulder.

". . . you started it . . ."

". . . *you* did . . ."

Doreen crushed her cigarette and lit another. She took one drag, then smashed it out in disgust. She put her hands on her knees and stared at them.

"What was an 'accident'?" I asked.

She started to speak, then closed her mouth. Her eyes never left the backs of her hands.

"Are you talking about Clare's death?"

She held perfectly still, not looking up.

"Mrs. Butler, if—"

"They can't make me testify, can they?" She wouldn't look at me, but I could see that her face was filled with fear.

"Testify to what?"

"A wife doesn't have to testify against her husband, does she?"

"No."

She kept staring at her hands. "I'm—I'm afraid to say this, but . . . and I love him, no matter what, but . . ."

I waited, knowing what was coming.

"Kenneth killed Clare," she said softly.

CHAPTER

27

WE SAT IN SILENCE for a moment. Her head hung as if she were in church and I were her confessor.

"Did Kenneth tell you he'd killed her?"

She shook her head, then looked up at me. "No. But I know he did it. I think I've always known. I just wouldn't let myself think about it. Perhaps because I could see no reason for Kenneth to— Until Thursday, when you came here and said Clare had hired a private detective to find Jeremy Stone. Then it made sense. I mean, the things that happened right before Clare was murdered."

"What happened?"

She heaved a sigh, and for the first time since I'd arrived, she seemed to relax, as if she'd finally accepted things as they were.

"Kenneth received a phone call the night before the murder. I was unloading the dishwasher, and he stretched the kitchen phone cord so he was standing just outside the doorway. I couldn't hear what he was saying, but I could tell he was angry. Arguing. He was upset for the rest of the night. I asked him about it, and he said it was 'a problem at work.'"

Samuel Butler had overheard Clare arguing with a man

on the phone that night. Not with her lover, though. With Kenneth.

Doreen said, "The next day, Kenneth had a similar call. Again, I couldn't hear what he was saying, only that he was very angry. He left the house right afterward. 'To solve a problem at work,' he said."

"What time was this?"

"Around eleven or so."

After Samuel Butler had left for Golden.

"Why was Kenneth home so late in the morning? I thought he worked on Saturdays."

"He does occasionally. Today, for instance, because there's a large order they're getting out."

"What time did he come home that day?"

"Late afternoon. Around four, I think." She bit her lip. "His face was pale, and he was very upset. Of course, I thought it had something to do with the company. I asked him, but he wouldn't talk about it. He told me if anyone asked, I was to say he'd been home all day. At the time, it didn't make sense. When I tried to question him, he just got angry. He made me swear to tell no one that he'd left the house. And that night, I heard about Clare."

"How did you hear?"

"Samuel came here and told us. I was shocked. Right then I should've connected Kenneth's behavior with Clare's death. But I didn't. I guess I wouldn't let myself. Now, though . . ." She gave me a pleading look. "I'm sure it was an accident. Kenneth would never intentionally harm anyone. But his temper . . . Sometimes he gets mad and does things, breaks things, and then he's immediately sorry. I—I suppose that's what happened. He didn't *mean* to kill her."

Explain that to Clare. "Call your husband now and tell him to come home. Then I'll phone Oliver Westfall. He should be here to counsel Kenneth before he turns himself in."

"I . . ."

"It's either that or you go to the police with this."

"No," she said quickly. "You told me I don't have to testify, and I won't."

"I said the court can't force you to testify. That's not the same as your volunteering."

"No, I—I can't."

"Are you forgetting that your father-in-law is in jail?"

I must've shouted, because she winced. Her eyes were rimmed with red and filling with tears.

"I . . ." She stood stiffly. "Excuse me, please," she said, and hurried from the room.

She disappeared down the hallway. A door closed.

I sat for what seemed a long time, staring at the empty room, trying to imagine the pain within Doreen. Finally, I walked to the kitchen, found the cupboard with the glasses, and got a drink of water.

The window over the sink offered a view of the backyard. There was a wide expanse of lawn and a lot of lilac bushes just beginning to show leaves. One corner of the yard was taken up by a mammoth jungle gym. The Butler tykes clambered over it, involved in some elaborate fantasy. Not unlike their parents.

I went back to the living room and sat down. A moment later, Doreen appeared, her eyes red but her tears gone. Her face was paler than before. She'd washed off her makeup.

I stood. "Are you ready to call Kenneth?"

"No."

"Look, Mrs. Butler—"

"I said *no*." She gave me a glare almost too brief to mention. "I will not disturb Kenneth at work."

"Excuse me?"

"Kenneth has an important order to get out. That's why he's working today. He'll be home sometime this afternoon. Then we can— Then you can talk to him about . . . everything."

MICHAEL ALLEGRETTO

Her mouth defined a thin, straight line. She was trying
her damnedest to stand firm, to maintain her dignity. Or
perhaps she just wanted to preserve the status quo as long
as possible.

"Mrs. Butler . . ."

"*No.*" Her voice was shrill.

I didn't want to push her. I needed her cooperation.
That is, Samuel Butler did. Because unless Doreen convinced Kenneth to turn himself in—or agreed to testify
against him—there was no way to prove he'd killed Clare.
Sure, he'd had a motive: Clare had found out about the
phantom employee, Jeremy Stone. Although now I wondered how she'd done it without the help of Gil Lucero;
he'd barely gotten started before he'd had his "accident."

Whatever the case, there was little if anything to tie
Kenneth to Clare's murder. My testimony as to what Doreen had just told me would be worthless—hearsay, inad-
missible. I had to get her to testify or to pressure Kenneth
into confessing. But pampering her by letting Kenneth
complete his workday? I don't think so.

"Listen to me," I said, getting parental, "either you call
your husband right now, or I will."

She blinked as if she'd been slapped. "You can't talk to
me like that."

"Make up your mind," I said. "And I mean now."

Her eyes filled again with tears. Lomax, you bully.

"I'll . . . call." Her voice was low and pathetic.

I followed her to the kitchen. She phoned Butler
Manufacturing and asked for Kenneth. She listened for a
few moments, requested that Kenneth phone her, and
hung up.

"He's gone to lunch with a customer," she said, looking
at the phone, not at me. "Alice doesn't know where they
went or when they'll be back."

Swell. Business before prosecution.

"All right, we'll do it this afternoon. Oliver Westfall should be here, too."

She nodded.

"Do you have his home phone number?"

"I—yes, I believe so."

She got out a small binder and flipped pages until she found the number. I copied it.

"Mrs. Butler, if Kenneth should come home without calling, maybe you'd better wait until Westfall and I get here before you confront him."

"Why? I *want* to talk to him alone."

"Yes, but you said he sometimes gets angry. It's possible he might—"

"No," she said firmly. "Kenneth would never hurt me. Never."

I had to assume that she knew what she was talking about. And really, my greatest concern wasn't that Kenneth would harm Doreen. He may have murdered Clare in a fit of rage, but he did it to protect his interests, which I believed included his family. No, my chief worry was that he'd convince Doreen to clam up, making it much more difficult for Westfall and me to convince him to admit his guilt and turn himself in.

Of course, he might run. But there wasn't a hell of a lot I could do to stop him—not legally, anyway.

"I'll come back this afternoon with Oliver Westfall," I said. "He can help only if Kenneth does the right thing."

"I—I know. Good-bye, Mr. Lomax."

She showed me out, then closed the door softly behind me, alone at last with her agony.

I drove to my office to phone Westfall. There was a message on my machine from Lieutenant MacArthur asking me to call him. He didn't say why.

I dialed Westfall first. He seemed annoyed that I had his home number.

"I've got good news and bad news," I said.

"I don't have time to play games, Mr. Lomax. My wife and I are just leaving for a luncheon with the Republican—"

"The good news is we can prove that Samuel Butler didn't murder Clare."

That got his attention. "Are you certain?"

"The bad news is your new client is Kenneth Butler."

"What are you saying?"

"Kenneth killed Clare."

"*What?* How do you know?"

As briefly as possible I filled him in on what I'd learned about Jeremy Stone and what Doreen Butler had confessed to me.

"Have you told any of this to the police?"

"No. I thought you should hear it first. Besides, there's little I can tell the cops that I can prove. We need to get Kenneth or Doreen to talk."

"Oh, I can manage that," he said heatedly. "I'll force Kenneth to surrender his books and hand them to the police. When they see his motive for killing Clare, they'll rake him and Doreen over the coals until one of them breaks."

"I see. So you won't represent Kenneth in court? "

"I will if he wants me to. At the moment, though, I represent Samuel Butler, and I'll do everything in my power to get him freed."

"Do you want to talk to Kenneth or not?"

"Of course."

"Could there be a conflict of interest?"

"You let me worry about that."

"Right. Look, I don't know when Kenneth's going to return, so—"

"I'll phone Doreen Butler now and tell her to call me here the minute she hears from him."

"What about your luncheon?"

"Screw the luncheon." He hung up.

I called police headquarters and was put on hold. Five minutes later, MacArthur came on the line.

"Hi, Pat, it's Jake."

"I want you to come in here."

"What, no hello?"

"Now. I'll send a squad car if you like."

"Hey, I can drive. What's up?"

"I have some pictures I want you to look at, see if you recognize anyone."

"Pictures of who?"

"Friends of William Royce."

CHAPTER

28

WHILE I RODE THE ELEVATOR up to MacArthur's floor,
I debated whether to tell him about Kenneth Butler.

I was still working for Westfall, though, and Westfall
was more or less Kenneth's attorney. So what I had was
privileged information, albeit hearsay. In times past, Mac-
Arthur and I could've spoken off the record about such
things, friend to friend. But I feared those times were
gone. MacArthur was grooming himself for promotion—a
company man. If I convinced him Kenneth Butler was
guilty, he'd never let him surrender on his own. He'd
send the troops after him. And while he was at it, he
might find some reason to lock *me* up, just to show everyone what a good cop he was.

I passed through the squad room, which wasn't nearly
as busy as the last time I'd been here. Of course, this was
Saturday. Even crooks need a day off.

The door to MacArthur's office was open. I knocked as
I walked in.

He was on the phone, listening more than speaking.
He waved me into a chair in front of his desk.

"All right, Chief," he said, "if that's what you want, I'll
see that it gets done. Count on it, Chief." He hung up.

"You forgot to say hi to your wife for me."

190

He didn't crack a smile, just the folder on his desk, all business. The good old days were dead.

"We've received information from California on William Royce," he said, scanning a page in his folder. "His last known employer was Frank Dykstra, a twice-convicted drug dealer. Over the years, Dykstra has dealt heroin, cocaine, and more recently, a drug called ice. Have you heard of it?"

"Vaguely."

"It's a pure form of methamphetamine that the user smokes rather than injects or eats. Addicts can go about their lives—school, job, whatever—for months before the drug catches up with them. Then it's paranoia and sometimes violence. In any case, ice was first smuggled into this country from Korea, and then labs began to show up in Hawaii, California, and Texas. That's where Dykstra comes in. He's got a nephew, Carl, same last name. The kid's a recent college graduate, chemistry degree. Frank's apparently taken him under his wing."

"Carl's cooking ice for his uncle Frank."

"It looks that way. The L.A. police believe the Dykstras were setting up an ice lab before running afoul of some Asian competition. Three Korean men were shot to death, and Frank and Carl disappeared. That was six months ago, and there's been no sign of them until you ran into William Royce last Wednesday."

"You think the Dykstras are in Denver?"

"It's possible, and if so, Frank might be setting up a lab. He'd keep Royce and others like him around for protection. Here he's got the bikers to worry about. Speed is a biker industry, and they might consider ice to be part of it."

He withdrew photos from the folder and set them on the desk, facing me.

There was a mug shot of Frank Dykstra, full face and

profile, holding a numbered placard under his chin. Chins. He was heavyset, around fifty, with a high forehead and one sleepy eye. He looked familiar. There was a series of photos, apparently taken with a long lens, showing Frank and Carl walking out of a building and getting into a car. Carl wore a bomber jacket and a nineties haircut—shaved on the sides and long in back. The last picture from MacArthur's folder was a posed shot of Carl in a cap and gown.

"Where'd this come from, the family album?"

"Do you know either of them?" MacArthur asked, all business.

I tapped Frank's mug shot with my finger. "I think I've seen him before."

"Where?"

"Driving the carload of shooters last Wednesday night at the golf course."

MacArthur's brow wrinkled. "Are you sure?"

"Not a hundred percent. The light was bad. But I think it was him."

"Then he's probably setting up an ice lab. Would you know anything about that?"

"No."

"Why would Dykstra want you dead?"

"I don't know."

"Don't you?" He gave me a look that cops are famous for: You're lying, and we both know it, so you might as well start telling the truth and ease your conscience.

"Hey, Pat, give it a rest, all right? There's only—"

"I asked you a question."

I'd been about to explain that there were only minor hints of ice in the Butler case: Clare Butler owned an ice pipe, Wes Hartman had admitted that he'd once smoked ice, and Samuel Butler's flower vendor was an ice addict. All of it was a long way from a hard-core drug operation and the Dykstra boys. And it was doubtful any of it would be useful to MacArthur. Still, I should've told him. But I was put off by his brand-new hard-ass attitude.

"No, I have no idea why Dykstra would want to kill me." That much, anyway, was the truth.

He gave me one last long, hard stare. Then he said, "Here," and handed me a voucher with his signature at the bottom. "Take that down to the property clerk and you can get your gun back."

I hesitated.

"Something you want to say?"

"I guess not."

"Then close the door on your way out."

Downstairs the property clerk gave me my .38 snubnose and a little plastic bag with the empty shells.

Walking out to the car I thought about William Royce and Frank and Carl Dykstra. After they'd tried to snuff me at the golf course—in fact, right up until this morning—I'd assumed their attempt was somehow tied to Clare's murder, part of a cover-up. But Kenneth had killed Clare. So if the shooters were covering up, they were working for Kenneth.

Somehow that seemed unlikely.

Kenneth had been stealing from his father, stealing for himself and his family. He'd committed one desperate, violent act to protect himself. But Royce and the Dykstras were another breed, involved in something else entirely. So why were they after me? Somewhere in the past few days I must've kicked over a rock and disturbed them. The question was, which rock?

I tried to put a name to it. Only one came to mind— Wes Hartman. Perhaps because he was the sole member of the Butler clan who'd smoked ice.

Well, there had been one other. Clare.

Had she been connected with the Dykstras?

On my way to the office I swung under some golden arches for lunch. Before I unwrapped everything, I phoned Doreen Butler. She still hadn't heard from Kenneth. I told her I'd wait by the phone for her call.

Halfway through my burger the phone rang. It wasn't Doreen, though, it was Karen.

"I need your help." She sounded upset. "I don't know who else to call."

"What's wrong?"

"I don't want to talk about it over the phone. Can you come to my house?"

"Now?"

"Please."

"Karen, I'm expecting an extremely important call, and if I'm not here to—"

"*This* is important."

"All right, calm down. If you'd just tell me—"

"It's my sister," she said.

"Nicole? What's wrong?"

"She's here. She says . . . she killed Clare."

CHAPTER

29

I CALLED WESTFALL and told him where I'd be without saying why. Then I drove to south Denver.

Karen lived on South Pearl Street in a quiet neighborhood of small brick bungalows and huge old elms. There was a new silver Subaru parked crookedly in front of her house, its right front tire over the curb.

I climbed the steps to the front porch and rang the bell.

Karen answered wearing tight blue jeans and a loose cotton pullover that wasn't quite as black as her hair. Worry lines divided her delicate eyebrows. Again I was struck by how little she resembled her father and her siblings, her facial bones more fragile, her eyes pale hazel, not dark brown. In fact, she hardly looked like a blood relative.

"Thanks for coming." She held the screen door open.

The living room was small and tidy and smelled of flowers. A pair of blue-and-white-striped love seats formed an L before a fireplace framed in rose and white tiles. The firebrick and inner hearth gleamed, and the andirons had been replaced by a porcelain cat. On the mantelpiece was a large cut-glass vase with a spray of white carnations.

"Where is she?"

"In the bedroom. I told her to lie down. I didn't know what else to do. When she came here, she was jumpy as hell, talking a mile a minute. She said she'd gotten in an argument with Clare and then sort of blacked out. The next thing she knew, she was in her car, driving home. There was blood on her clothes. At home she told Wes she didn't know what had happened. He explained that she'd killed Clare and that they were to keep it a secret."

"Let me talk to her."

I followed Karen through the room to a closed door on the left. She put her hand on the doorknob and turned to me.

"She might be asleep," she said softly.

I nodded, and she opened the door. "Nicole?"

I went in behind her. The bed was empty, the bedspread rumpled. Karen turned right, and I followed her through a long bathroom with an old black-and-white-tiled floor, a bathtub standing on clawed feet, a shoulder-high cedar bureau, and a freestanding white sink with separate spigots for hot and cold water. There was another door at the end of the bathroom, hanging open, leading into the kitchen.

"Nicole?" Karen called, panic in her voice.

I had to jog to keep up with her through the kitchen and out the back door.

At the rear of the yard was a detached two-car garage. The side door stood open. Karen ran for it.

Karen's white Miata was parked inside with the top up. Nicole sat behind the wheel, struggling to get the key in the ignition. She looked up and saw us, terrified, and fought more than ever to work the key. I don't know where she thought she was going; the garage door was closed and manually operated. She'd have to get out of the car to open it.

Karen hurried around to the driver's side and pulled on the door. It was locked.

"Nicole, please come out." She'd spoken loud enough to be heard through the closed side window but still managed to keep her tone gentle. "We want to help you, honey. Please."

Nicole continued to fight with the key. Then suddenly she stopped and pressed her forehead to the steering wheel, eyes closed, lips moving soundlessly. Karen pleaded with her to unlock the door. Finally, Nicole did so, slowly, as if she were in a trance.

Karen helped her out of the car.

Nicole's face was very pale. Her eyes were half-closed, and the lids were so dark they looked bruised. She was dressed the way I'd seen her at her condo Tuesday night—black tights, black running shoes, and a billowy long-sleeved man's shirt spattered with paint.

Karen put her arm around her little sister's shoulder and led her toward the doorway. I stood out of the way. Nicole was babbling.

". . . I killed her, Wes said I killed her, don't let them hurt me, Karen I didn't mean to, Wes said so and he'll leave me if I tell and Daddy will be in prison and I'll be all alone and I don't remember doing it but Wes said so, and he said we mustn't tell and, oh Karen, if he leaves me I'll be all alone Karen don't let him . . ."

"Sh, honey, it'll be all right."

Nicole leaned heavily against her sister, who led her from the garage. Nicole didn't even know I was there. She seemed to sag more with each step, and by the time the three of us had gone through the house to the bedroom, she was dead on her feet. I helped Karen lay her on the queen-size bed. We removed Nicole's shoes and covered her with a quilt. Karen sat beside her, stroking her hair, whispering, telling her everything would be all right.

I felt intrusive, and I turned to leave. Something on the chest of drawers caught my eye.

It was a glass pipe, like the one I'd found in Clare's room. Beside it was a vial with several lumps of what looked like sea salt. Ice. Also on the bureau was a framed photograph of Karen standing beside a pretty young woman with long blond hair. She and Karen were nicely dressed, posing in a studio, their bodies partly turned to each other. They were holding hands.

The woman reminded me a bit of Clare. And I remembered that Clare had lived here for a month when she first came to Denver.

I noticed Karen watching me.

She stood up from the bed and spoke softly. "She's asleep. Let's leave her alone for a while."

We sat in the living room on our separate love seats. There were two cats in the fireplace now. The porcelain one stayed put, and the other, a sleek calico, crept up to my feet and sniffed my pant cuff.

"Where'd you get the pipe?" I asked, startling the cat. It leapt up on the seat beside Karen.

"You had no right to snoop around in there," she said, her voice shaded with anger.

"I wasn't snooping."

"And if you're wondering about the photograph—"

"I'm not."

"—it's Teri, the woman who works for me. We're lovers." She gave me a defiant look.

"Swell. Now what about the pipe?"

Some of the anger went out of her. She looked down at the cat and ran her fingers along its back. It's tail stood straight up.

"Nicole brought it with her. I hate that shit."

"Ice?"

"Drugs, period. Look how screwed up it's got her." Karen shook her head and grinned crookedly. "She was trying to start my Miata with the key to her Subaru." The smile left her. Gently, she lifted the cat and laid it over her shoulder, as if she were burping a baby. She stroked it, staring vacantly at the cold cat in the fireplace.

"How long has Nicole been here?"

"An hour or so."

"Did she call first?"

"No. I answered the door, and there she was. It surprised me, because she rarely visits. She hasn't been here in months."

"What else did she tell you about the murder?"

"I could barely understand her. I let her in, and she started pacing around the room, very jittery, rambling on about how mad Daddy would be. I asked her why he'd be mad, and she just jabbered about our childhood, our mother, how Clare never belonged, and so on. I tried to get her to calm down, to lie down. She said she hadn't been to bed since Monday—four nights without sleep. It frightened me. It's that damn drug she's been smoking. She said Wes gives it to her. She tried to light up when she got here. I took it away from her and made her lie down. And that's when she told me what she'd done. That she'd killed Clare."

The cat moved, and Karen let it go. It tightroped along the back of the love seat, then stretched out on its belly and closed its eyes.

"I didn't know what to do, whether to take her to a hospital or call the police. I'm afraid of what will happen to her."

"Nicole didn't kill Clare."

Karen looked at me in disbelief. Or maybe it was restrained hope. "But you heard her admit it."

"She doesn't remember killing Clare, only that Wes told her so. He's got her convinced that she did it."

"What? No. Nicole wouldn't admit something like that just because Wes told her."

"Maybe not normally. But how long has she been smoking ice? Since she's been married to Wes? That drug can play serious tricks with the mind. And I'll bet that ever since the murder Wes has been keeping her well supplied."

"But could he make her *believe* it?"

"Perhaps."

"That fucking asshole."

"Exactly."

"Why would he do it?"

"I don't know for sure. Maybe to control her. Maybe to keep your father in jail."

She blinked once. "What do you mean?"

"Wes may be stealing from Butler Manufacturing. Whatever he's doing, he probably feels freer with Samuel out of the way."

"Then . . . did Wes kill Clare?"

"No."

"Then my father . . ."

"Not him, either."

She looked at me, waiting.

"Brace yourself. It was your brother."

"Kenneth?"

I filled her in on what I'd learned about Jeremy Stone and what Doreen had confessed to me. She was stunned. Hey, who wouldn't be? In the span of a few hours she'd believed that first her father, then her sister, and now her brother had murdered Clare.

"What are we going to do about Nicole?"

"She definitely needs help," I said. "For now, though, I think you're right—let her sleep. When she wakes up, we'll talk to her and figure out what to do."

The phone rang in the kitchen.

Karen went to answer it, then came back and said, "It's Oliver Westfall."

When I picked up the receiver, Westfall told me, "Doreen Butler just called. Kenneth's on his way home."

CHAPTER

30

I TOLD KAREN TO KEEP NICOLE there until I returned. It didn't seem prudent to let her go home to Wes. When he found out Nicole was confiding in us, his reaction would be in direct proportion to the size of the secret he was hiding. He might try to shut Nicole up—forever.

"I'm not sure when I'll be back. If Wes should come here before I—"

"Don't worry," she said. "I can handle Wes."

"I don't want you to handle him. Don't let him in. If he won't go away, call the police."

"The police? But what if Nicole starts babbling about Clare's murder?"

"Right now Wes is a greater threat to Nicole than the police."

I walked out and heard her lock the front door and slide the chain in place.

There were no cars in front of Kenneth's house or in the driveway. Westfall hadn't yet arrived. I debated whether to wait for him or go in now. He was the one to counsel Kenneth. On the other hand, if Doreen were now confronting her husband, Kenneth might be reaching for a blunt instrument.

I climbed out of the Toyota.

A car turned the corner and approached me from behind—a brand-new shiny black Jaguar Vanden Plas. I guess law school was paying off. The Jag parked a cautionary distance behind my grubby ride, and Oliver Westfall got out. He was dressed for business—a taupe-gray double-breasted suit, white shirt, dark tie.

"Has Kenneth arrived yet?" he asked me as we started up the walk together.

"I just got here myself."

I rang the bell, then stepped aside for the man in the suit.

Kenneth Butler answered the door in a dress shirt and suspenders. He looked surprised to see us. "What are you two doing here?"

I guess Doreen hadn't delivered the bad news.

Westfall said, "May we come in?"

Doreen was in the living room, lighting a cigarette with nervous hands.

Kenneth looked a question at her, saying, "It's Westfall and Lomax."

"Maybe I . . . should see about the children." She started to leave the room.

Westfall stopped her with "You should be here for this, Mrs. Butler."

"What's he talking about?" Kenneth asked his wife. "What are you talking about, Oliver?"

"Perhaps we should all sit down."

Doreen dropped immediately on the couch. Westfall motioned to Kenneth to have a seat beside her. He hesitated, then sat. Westfall took the easy chair, and I remained standing in the doorway, the trusty sergeant at arms.

"Now what's this all about?" Kenneth demanded, trying to act as if he didn't have a clue. But there was sweat along his hairline.

"First of all," Westfall said, "I'm here as your friend and, if you like, your legal counsel."

"Legal—"

"Anything said here will be held in strict confidence. Secondly, I truly want to help you, but I can do so only if you're completely honest with me."

"I don't know what the hell you're talking about." Kenneth's tone was even, but red splotches had appeared on his face, betraying inner conflict.

Westfall sighed. "Kenneth, we know about the deceased Mr. Jeremy Stone and how you've been using him to take money from the company."

Kenneth glared at Westfall, the splotches spreading. Now his entire face was an ugly shade of red. "How did—" Then he turned on Doreen. She seemed to sink into the couch beside him.

"*You?*"

"Kenneth, I . . ." Her voice was barely audible.

"God*damn* you!" he shouted, coming to his feet, banging against the coffee table, towering over Doreen. "Jeremy Stone was *your* idea! And now you're informing on *me*?" He shook his left fist at her, index finger extended in accusation. Then he raised his right hand as if to slap her. "I ought to—"

I moved quickly behind him and caught his wrist. He redirected his rage, whirling toward me, jerking his wrist free, and swinging his left fist in an overhand arc. I leaned out of the way, and he connected with nothing but air. His momentum carried him across the coffee table, and he went down on it, breaking one slim cherry-wood leg with a snap like a pistol shot. He scrambled up from his hands and knees, charging at me in a crouch, head raised, face blood black with hatred.

I got a glimpse of Doreen on the couch, hands covering her mouth, holding in a scream. Westfall had jumped to his feet, but that's as far as he was going.

I backpedaled away from Kenneth, knocked over a table lamp, caught it, stepped aside as he lunged at me, and hit him with it. Not too hard, just enough to distract him. He stumbled past, reaching for me. I grabbed his arm, twisted it behind him, and slammed him into the wall. He threw himself back, flailing wildly with his free arm, and we danced around the room until I hooked his foot with my heel and dropped him facedown on the carpet, hard enough to rattle the windows. His nose was bleeding, but if anything, he fought harder than before, so I caught his thumb in a come-along hold and applied just enough pressure to make him roar like a bear.

"Hold still or I'll break your goddamn hand," I apprised him.

And suddenly someone was pulling my hair and pummeling me with tiny fists.

"Get off my daddy!"

"Leave my daddy alone!"

The Butler tykes to the rescue. And now I felt completely ridiculous, as if we were all involved in a friendly family free-for-all. Doreen hurried over, and for a moment I thought it was four against one. But she pulled her children from me and took them, yelling, out of the room.

Kenneth fought beneath me, arching his back, raising us both off the floor. I wasn't sure how much longer I could hold him, and if I let him up, fists would fly. I put more pressure on his thumb and suggested that he hold still. For a reply, he tried to claw at my face with his free hand.

"Westfall, go out to my car and—dammit, Butler, I swear to God I'll break your hand—there's a pair of handcuffs in the glove compartment."

He just stared at me.

"Move it. Unless you want to hold him for me."

Westfall moved. He returned in a minute with the cuffs. I slapped a bracelet on one of Butler's wrists, no problem. If Westfall were the physical type, we could've

wrestled Kenneth's other arm behind him. But handing
me the cuffs had been as rough as the lawyer would get.
He watched us from a safe distance.

I told Kenneth to put his other arm behind him. He
called me a few nasty names and tried again to claw at
me over his shoulder, so I leaned on his thumb until he
cried out. He squeezed his eyes, gritted his teeth, and
fought the pain. Finally, he couldn't take it anymore. He
let me cuff him.

I climbed off his back and tried to help him up. He
shrugged me off, lying there, out of breath. I tucked in
my shirt and straightened my jacket, breathing a bit hard
myself. Finally, Kenneth rolled over and sat up on the
floor, hands behind him. His lower face was smeared with
nose blood.

"I'll get you for this, you son of a bitch." He spat blood
on the carpet and got to his feet, wobbling. "If it's the
last thing I do, I'll get you."

"Assuming they ever let you out of prison," I said.

He sneared. "For what I did? I'm a family man with
absolutely no criminal record. I'll probably get a fine and
probation."

"If all you'd done was steal, maybe. But the court's a
bit harsher when it comes to murder."

"Murder?" His face slowly lost its color. Except for the
blood glistening on his chin and the red lump on his
forehead, where I'd tapped him with the lamp. "No. I
had nothing to do with Winks getting killed."

Westfall and I exchanged a glance.

"We're speaking of Clare's murder," Westfall told him.

"Clare? You think *I* killed Clare?"

"I'm sorry, Kenneth, I had to tell them."

We all turned to see Doreen Butler standing in the
doorway. She was twisting her wedding ring, screwing it
on tighter.

"For your father's sake." She moaned. "Oh, God, Kenneth, you know I love you and—"

"Wait a minute." Kenneth was shaking his head, a pained expression on his face. "What the hell is going on here?"

"Perhaps we should all sit down," Westfall said, ready to start over as if nothing had happened. And really, the only difference was that some of the furniture was disarranged and Kenneth wore handcuffs, no big deal. "Doreen, get something for Kenneth's face. Please, Kenneth, sit."

I put the lamp back in place and righted the cherry-wood coffee table on its three remaining legs. Kenneth sat on the couch and let Doreen wipe his face with a damp towel. He glared at me.

"Take these damn things off."

"Maybe later," I told him.

Westfall said, "Tell us about you and Clare."

"I didn't kill her, if that's what you mean."

Westfall waited. Kenneth gave him a tight-lipped stare. Westfall soaked it up. Kenneth sighed and looked away, shrugging his shoulders.

"Clare confronted me about Jeremy Stone," he said. "I should've seen it coming—or known that *something* was coming—because a few weeks before that, an employee told me someone named Gil Lucero was asking questions about Stone. I didn't know who Lucero was or what he was up to, but I was worried. It must've shown at work, because Wes asked me what was wrong, said maybe he could help. I told him Lucero was poking his nose where it didn't belong, that's all I said. Wes told me not to worry, that he'd take care of it."

"So he ran over Lucero with a truck."

Kenneth looked at me. "I didn't know about that until you told me a few days ago. I thought Wes was just going to *talk* to the guy."

MICHAEL ALLEGRETTO

"Did Wes drive the truck, or was it someone else?"

"I don't know. I told you, I didn't know anything about it."

Obviously, Wes wasn't driving when I'd nearly been run over. But my guess was he'd set it up.

"Can we return to the point here?" Westfall directed.

"Anyway," Kenneth said, "soon after that, Clare confronted me. She said she knew I was stealing from the company and that Jeremy Stone was helping me and if I didn't cut her in she'd tell my father. I could see she didn't really know who Stone was. It didn't matter, though. If my father had a reason to study the books and started asking about Jeremy Stone, I'd be screwed."

"Did Wes know about Stone?" I asked.

"No."

"Did you tell him about Clare's threats?"

"I didn't tell anyone. I felt I had only one choice—pay her."

"You gave Clare money?" Doreen asked, shocked. Money meant a lot to her.

Kenneth nodded.

"How much?"

"Ten thousand."

"Ten— And just where did you get ten thousand dollars?"

"I cashed in one of our CDs."

"*What?*" Now Doreen was pissed. And Kenneth was open to attack, his hands pinned behind him. I got ready to restrain her. Well, maybe I'd let her slap him just once. "Why didn't you tell me about that?" she demanded.

"I didn't want to upset you." He gave her a sorrowful look, and she glared at him. Now wasn't that sweet? They were sharing, switching roles. "Besides," Kenneth went on, "I knew Jeremy Stone would make us the money back in a few months. But then . . . well, she wanted more.

She phoned here the evening before the murder. We argued. She threatened me, swore she'd tell my father if I didn't bring her another ten thousand. I told her I needed time. She called back the next morning, and we argued some more. I left the house in a rage. I was ready to go over there and wring her neck. Thank God I cooled down. I drove around for a while, then went to the office. I seriously considered destroying the books. Instead, I wrote her a personal check and took it to her.

"But when I got to my father's house, there were police cars parked in front, and all the neighbors were in the street. One of them told me a woman had been murdered. It scared the hell out of me. I drove straight home without knowing what had happened. I didn't want to know, didn't want to be involved." He faced Doreen. "That's why I told you to lie for me, to say I'd been home all day if anyone asked."

No one said anything.

Kenneth looked at each of us, seeking acceptance.

"That's what happened," he said. "I swear to God I didn't kill her."

I think I believed him. Westfall raised his eyebrows at me and said, "Back to square one."

"Not quite. There's Wes Hartman."

CHAPTER

31

THEY ALL LOOKED AT ME.

Westfall said, "Are you saying Wes killed Clare?"

I pictured Nicole, hallucinating on ice, spattered with her paints, and Wes telling her, Yes, that's Clare's blood, and you killed her.

"Perhaps."

"But why?"

"I don't know. Maybe she was trying to blackmail him as well as Kenneth." I turned to Kenneth. "Wes killed Winks, though, didn't he? Or had him killed."

Kenneth shook his head and tried to look innocent. "I don't know anything about that."

"You knew he was murdered."

He smiled weakly. "Doesn't everyone?"

"The police version is suicide."

Kenneth's smile sank.

"I guess Hartman was the answer to all your problems," I said. "First Gil Lucero, then Clare—"

"I didn't *tell* him about—"

"—a couple of shots at me, then Winks."

"No," he said firmly. "No, that's *not* how it was."

"How was it?"

Kenneth glanced from me to Westfall to Doreen, looking for an ally. Doreen had moved away from him on the

210

couch. Now she said quietly but evenly, "Yes, Kenneth, tell us how it was."

He was surrounded, scared witless. Good.

"Did you sic Wes on Winks?" I asked.

"No, no, I . . . *told* him about Winks, that's all."

"What did you tell him?"

"That Winks was crucial to my father's defense."

"Why did you tell him?"

"Why?"

"Yes. Were you hoping he'd make sure Winks wouldn't testify?"

"*What?* Why would I do that? I *love* my father. The last thing I want is for him to go to prison."

"That's . . . not quite true." This from Doreen.

Kenneth turned to her. "What are you saying?"

"You told me you hoped he'd be convicted."

"No."

"You hated him, Kenneth, for the way he—"

"Shut up, Doreen."

"—the way he abused you and your mother and Karen. The way he spoiled Nicole. And besides, with him out of the way you could—"

"*Shut up!*"

"—you could run the company. And that's all you ever wanted."

"I SAID SHUT UP!"

He was on his feet again, towering over her, his face blotchy red. This time, though, Doreen sat erect and didn't shrink from him. She didn't even blink. Maybe because his hands were cuffed behind him. Or maybe she was really seeing him for the first time. Herself, too.

"Sit down, Kenneth," she said with scorn. "You look ridiculous."

He puffed up his chest as if he were ready to let go with another shout. Slowly, though, he deflated and sat at the end of the couch, defeated.

No one spoke. I glanced at Westfall. He was staring at Kenneth, unsure how to proceed.

I asked Kenneth, "When did you tell Wes about Winks?"

He shook his head, staring dully at the floor. "I don't remember." Doreen reached over and tentatively laid her hand on his knee. Now she felt sorry for him, her long-lost third child.

I said, "Your father told me he mentioned Winks to you when you visited the jail Tuesday."

Kenneth nodded, staring at Doreen's hand as if he wanted to hold it.

"Did you tell Wes that day?"

He frowned, still staring at Doreen's hand on his knee. Then he looked up at me.

"The next morning," he said. "Wes asked me about you, about how your investigation was proceeding. I told him you'd found Winks."

And that night William Royce and friends had tried to kill me. By that time they'd probably already silenced Winks.

"When I heard last night that Winks was dead," Kenneth said, "I knew it wasn't a coincidence. I knew Wes had something to do with it."

"We should take this to the police," Westfall suggested.

"Take what?" I faced him. "All we have on Wes Hartman are suspicions and innuendos. We need something concrete." I was thinking, Why would Wes want Winks dead? Answer: to keep Samuel Butler locked up and away from Butler Manufacturing. But why? I asked Kenneth, "Did Wes know you were stealing money from the company?"

He pressed his lips together and shook his head tightly, uncomfortable about admitting his crime.

"Could he be stealing, too?"

Kenneth frowned. "Do you mean money? No way."

"What about merchandise?"

"Well, we've got some minor pilfering. A few ballpoint pens and belt buckles always show up missing from inventory. Nothing major."

I recalled Hartman's actions last night when I'd broken into the building. My view had been partly blocked, but I could see that Wes had taken something from an outgoing shipment, put it in his gym bag, and left with it.

"What exactly does Hartman do for your company?"

"Very little." He winced and rolled his shoulders, flexing his arms behind him. I suppose I could've uncuffed him. But things were going so smoothly I hated to break his rhythm. "He services a few established customers and supposedly brings in new accounts, although he's done very little of that until recently."

"How recently?"

Kenneth pursed his lips. "In the past few months he's gotten us new customers in Kansas City, Minneapolis, and Omaha."

"Large accounts?"

"Well, no, but . . ."

"What?"

"Now that you mention it, they are unusual. Each of them orders fairly frequently, once a week or two. And always our cheapest merchandise—plastic mugs, and so on, not even with emblems."

I thought back to yesterday when I'd questioned the shipping clerk. He'd told the other worker, Molly, that the shipment she was working on, cheap plastic mugs, was going out tomorrow—that is, today—to a company in Minneapolis. And last night I'd seen Wes messing around with the boxes. It took me long enough, but I think I finally had it figured out.

"Is one of Wes's accounts Northfield Distributing in Minneapolis?"

Kenneth frowned. "Yes, but how did—"

213

"A shipment went out to them today."

"Well, yes. But how did you know?"

Dumb luck. "Thorough investigation. Have you ever heard Wes mention the names Frank or Carl Dykstra?"

"Dykstra?" He shook his head. "No. Although . . ."

"What?"

"He's meeting someone tonight named Frank. I overheard him today on the phone."

I felt my palms itch. "Where are they meeting?"

"I don't know. When I walked in this morning, he was talking, and when he saw me, he said, 'Got to go, Frank, see you tonight.' Then he hung up."

"Is Wes still at work?"

"No. He left before I did."

I knew that Wes would eventually go home, if he wasn't there already, and find Nicole gone. At some point he'd worry and start looking for her, probably calling around first. I didn't want him to get nervous and cancel his meeting with Frank.

I took the cuffs off Kenneth. He rubbed his wrists and gave me an apologetic look, I suppose for putting me through the trouble.

"Then you believe me?" he said. "That I didn't kill Clare?"

"Sure." The only thing I believed was that he wouldn't hit anybody or run away.

Doreen said, "Kenneth I—I'm sorry for what I thought I . . ."

"It's all right." He reached out for her. Lovely. A pair of thieves consoling each other.

I said to Kenneth, not ready to let him off the hook, "On the day of Clare's murder, when you drove to the house, where did you plan to park?"

He stopped petting and cooing with Doreen and gave me a confused look. "I don't know what you mean."

"If the cops hadn't been there, where would you have left your car?"

He shrugged. "In the driveway, I suppose?"

"Not in the garage?"

"No, how could I?"

"But if you would've left it in the driveway, the neighbors would've seen it."

He scowled. "Yes, I suppose so. I guess I wasn't thinking about that."

"You have a key to the front door, right?"

"Well, yes, but—"

"Who else could've let themselves in?"

"Nicole, for one," Doreen said bitterly, coming to his rescue. "She lived in that house right up until Clare moved in. Daddy's little girl would never give up her key."

"Karen has one, too," Kenneth said.

"That's what I thought."

Westfall looked at me. "Surely you don't think Karen had anything to do with this."

I ignored him and said to Kenneth, "Wes may phone or come here today looking for Nicole. I want Doreen to stay out of sight and for you to talk to him."

"Me? What am I supposed to say?"

"Tell him Nicole and Doreen went shopping together and possibly to dinner and that you don't expect them home until tonight. You're not worried about their absence. Do you understand? And if Wes asks how Nicole was acting, tell him she seemed fine."

"What's this all about?" Westfall wanted to know.

"I'm keeping Nicole away from Wes and trying not to make him suspicious."

"Where is Nicole?"

"Someplace safe." I hoped. I was counting on Karen's love for her baby sister as insurance against harm. I stood

215

and said to Westfall, "I've got things to take care of. As far as I'm concerned, the theft by these two supercrooks is a family matter, unless Samuel decides to press charges. You are going to tell him, aren't you?"

"Without question." He stared hard at Kenneth and Doreen. They hung their heads like penitents. "First I want to see the company's books so I can give him a full report. He may very well instruct me to inform the police. Or something equally appropriate."

I supposed he meant setting them adrift in the sea of unemployment. And I could see that Kenneth and Doreen feared that as much as jail. Ah, life in the middle class.

CHAPTER

32

THE FIRST THING I DID was rent a two-year-old blue Ford Tempo.

As far as I knew, Wes had never seen my borrowed, smoky, wheezy Toyota. But it was no good for tailing—too ugly to be indistinct. I peeled the rental agency's sticker from the Ford's front bumper, and the car practically disappeared into the background.

I swung by the office to pick up my state-of-the-art surveillance instruments—binoculars and a big thermos.

Before I left, I phoned Karen.

"Has Wes called?"

"Yes, just a little while ago. I told him I hadn't seen Nicole."

"How did he sound?"

"A bit worried, I think."

"How's Nicole?"

"Still sleeping, thank God. I think that's what she needs more than anything."

"Right." There was something else I wanted to ask her, but I didn't think now was the time.

"What?" she asked at my silence.

"We can talk about it later."

"Talk about what?" Her voice was flat, hard.

"All right. I'm curious. When Clare stayed with you for

a month, back when she first moved to Denver, how did she and Teri get along?"

A long pause. "They didn't."

"I see."

"What're you getting at?"

"Nothing." Much. "Make sure Nicole stays there until you hear from me, Westfall, or the police, even if it's not until tomorrow. And don't let her hurt herself. Do you understand what I'm saying?"

"She's my little sister," she said angrily. "You don't have to tell me how to take care of her."

At a convenience store I bought a bag of granola bars and filled the thermos with coffee. I was going to have to stick with Wes until his meeting with Frank, sometime tonight, which I figured was anytime between six o'clock and midnight. It was three now.

I drove south on University Boulevard, turned left on Yale, then left again into the alley that ran behind Wes and Nicole's condo. There was a large open space beside the condo, surrounded by a construction fence. Beyond it was an apartment building. Houses hid behind high privacy fences across the alley.

I swung the Ford around and parked near a dumpster between the apartment and the construction site. From there I could see the mouth of the driveway that led from the alley to the Hartman's building.

I climbed out, walked down the alley to the condo, and peeked through the garage-door window. The parking slots reserved for the residents of 2B were empty. No blood-red Nissan. I had to hope that Wes would come home before his meeting with Frank.

I sat in my car and waited.

My mind kept drifting back to Clare's murder.

The scene of the crime had been tidy, even peaceful— except, of course, for the body and the blood. No signs

218

of a break-in or a struggle. So Clare knew her killer, trusted him. Samuel Butler had been certain it was her lover. I'd thought he was right when I'd believed her lover was Jeremy Stone. But there was no Jeremy Stone. In any case, whoever the killer was, he probably had access to the house, possibly a key to the front door. And Clare must've been accustomed to him going into the garage, because that's where he'd picked up the murder weapon.

Unless he'd initially entered the house from the garage.

The garage.

I sat up straight, seeing the obvious, realizing what I should've known from the beginning. But I had to make sure. And I didn't think I was patient enough to wait for Wes before I checked it out.

I started the Ford and hoped that if Wes came home while I was gone, he'd stay awhile.

It was only a ten-minute drive to Samuel Butler's house. I parked at the curb, then let myself in with the key Westfall had given me last Monday. It seemed like a month ago.

The air in the house felt dead, as if all the oxygen had settled to the floor. I pictured it swirling about my ankles and rising in wisps as I moved through the living room and kitchen to the three-car garage.

Samuel's white Caddy and Clare's midnight-blue Porsche had not been moved. I took the garage-door opener from Clare's car and pressed the button. The overhead motor came to life, and the door behind the Porsche rolled smoothly up. I pushed the button again, and the door rolled down.

I raised the door behind the Caddy with Samuel's opener, then walked down the driveway to my car. After I got in, started the engine, and began to drive away, I pressed the button. The garage door rolled smoothly closed.

I drove to Wes's condo, parked in the alley, and walked back to check the garage. Still no red Nissan. Either Wes hadn't come home, or he'd come and gone.

I waited.

It was six-thirty when I saw the red Nissan enter the alley from Yale and turn into the driveway behind the condo. I unwrapped my third granola bar and sipped more coffee—not too much, though, or I'd have to go stand behind the dumpster.

I was beside the car stretching my legs in the chilly night air when Wes drove the Nissan out of the driveway, down the alley, and turned right onto Yale. It was nine-ten.

I fired up the Ford and went after him.

He led me north on University Boulevard. Traffic was moderate, so I could stay fairly close to him and still keep two or three cars between us. When he reached I-25, he took the northbound ramp, and I swung around behind him. The mountains were indistinct shapes to the west, crouching beyond the reach of the city glow.

Wes drove fast. I guess it would be hard not to, a car like that. Or maybe he was late for his meeting. In any case, I had to work to keep up with him as he continually changed lanes to move through traffic. I didn't try to get too close, though, remembering the last time I'd followed him.

I'd been rusty, careless, driving my shiny aqua-and-white antique. How could he *not* have spotted me. He'd used his car phone, setting things up. Then he'd driven to My Brother's Bar and stood on the sidewalk where I could see him, waving to make sure I'd stop—while the truck with the oversized tires sat up the hill a block away, waiting.

Wes took the Speer Boulevard exit, heading away from the city, just as he'd done when I'd followed him before. Had he spotted me again?

I let him pull ahead and watched his taillights turn north on Zuni, then east on Twenty-ninth Avenue, heading back toward downtown. He angled off onto Fifteenth Street and went down the hill toward My Brother's Bar. The skyscrapers hung in the background like gawkers at the scene of a crime.

I slowed the Ford, staying a few blocks back, waiting for him to stop.

But he continued past the bar, crossed the river, turned left, and disappeared.

I cruised down the hill and killed my lights, thinking he'd parked by one of the deserted buildings. But there was a cross street, Grinell Court, and I saw the Nissan's taillights a few hundred yards away.

The road was dark and lumpy, a two-lane blacktop that snaked under the Sixteenth Street viaduct and paralleled the Platte River, partially hidden by black foliage along the banks. To my right were warehouses and fence-enclosed storage lots, backed by the sprawling railroad yards. Beyond were the distant lights of civilization.

Wes's brake lights went on. The Nissan nearly stopped, then turned right, away from the river, carefully leaving the blacktop and going through an opening in a chain-link fence.

I pulled the Ford off the road, killed the engine, and climbed out.

It was dark and damp down here, as if the river were filling the night with its vapors. Hidden to my left, beyond the riverbank's trees, I-25 hummed quietly, the only sound. To my right were the black shapes of warehouses, blocking out the lights of downtown, a mile away.

I moved as quickly as I could along the edge of the road, trying to avoid the deeper shadows and ankle-turning potholes.

Ahead was a two-story brick cube with window lights on the first floor. The building sat thirty or forty feet

221

from the road, flanked on both sides by flat, open, weedy
ground. The entire area was bordered by a high chain-
link fence topped with razor wire.

The gate in the fence hung open, and I moved through
it to the front of the building. There was a steel door
secured with a couple of no-nonsense locks. The windows
on either side were painted out and covered with iron
bars.

I put my ear to the door.

Silence.

I stepped around the corner of the building to the
gravel drive that led to the back. The windows along this
side were head high and free of bars, the glass painted
white. The ones toward the rear of the building glowed
with light. They were open at the top. I could hear a
murmur of voices. And there was something else—an
odor. Faint, bitter.

I peeked around the corner.

Three vehicles were parked back there, end to end,
out of sight of the road. I knew them all. Wes's red Nissan
was behind a new Thunderbird, dark blue or black, just
like the one I'd seen a few nights ago at the golf course.
In front of the T-Bird was the notorious pickup truck on
oversized tires.

I unholstered the Magnum and stepped around the
corner.

A steel door was set in the rear of the building, flanked
by barred, painted-out windows. I went up a few concrete
steps to the door, put my head to it, and listened.

I heard a couple of distinct clicks.

From behind me.

The man stood about ten feet away, spotlighted by the
pale glow from the windows. He was a tall, skinny character with slicked-back hair, a zipped-up nylon jacket, and
a twelve-gauge pump shotgun. He must have been hiding
behind the vehicles, or maybe just back there catching a

smoke. A lit cigarette hung from his lip. It moved when he talked.

"Drop the gun, motherfucker, or I'll blow your fucking head off."

Some choice. I dropped the pistol.

CHAPTER

33

SKINNY TOLD ME to face the door and put my hands on my head. I heard him pick up the Magnum from where it had clattered to the bottom of the concrete steps.

"What the fuck're you doing here?"

"Meter reader."

"Fucking wise guy. Who are you?"

"I'm a friend of Wes. And Frank. But if they're busy now, I can come back later."

He jabbed me in the back with the muzzle of the shotgun. "Inside."

I swung open the steel door, and he shoved me in. A narrow hallway with a bare wooden floor ran straight through the building to the front. There were a few doors on either side, all closed except for the nearest one on the left. Light spilled from it into the hall.

"Through there," Skinny told me.

I stepped through the doorway. The odor I'd detected outside was stronger in here, though not as potent as I would've expected from a speed lab. Progress through chemistry.

There was little furniture in the room, making it seem spacious—a few chairs and a couple of long tables, one at each end. The table to my right was crowded with an apparatus of glass tubing, plus big brown glass jars with screw-on lids and huge glass beakers filled with pale white liquid.

Skinny ushered me around to the far end of the other table.

Four men were seated there, three of whom I knew. None looked happy to see me.

Wes Hartman, shocked and frightened, sat to my left beside a squat, broad-shouldered character with a shiny dome surrounded by a long, shaggy fringe of hair. Sitting across from them, their backs to the door, were Frank and Carl Dykstra, who looked a lot like their photographs—Frank heavy, Carl young.

"Who's this?" Frank demanded, angry. I guess he hadn't seen my face that night at the golf course.

"Found him nosing around outside," Skinny said from behind me.

"Lomax, what are you doing here?" Wes's voice quavered.

"Hi, Wes." I let my hands drop slowly to my sides. "Nice to see you again."

Frank looked at once surprised and pleased. "So this is Lomax."

Squatty said, "He don't look so tough to me." He stood up, all five and a half feet of him. But he had a shotgun, so I guess that made up for it. The light gleamed off the top of his head. "Not tough at all."

"Oh, really?" Frank said. "You missed him twice, once with the truck and once at the golf course."

Squatty's dome turned pink. "Yeah, well, I wasn't alone the second time. You and Royce were—"

"That's enough." Frank turned his bulk toward me. His bulging yellow shirt and dull green sports coat made him look like a giant toad. He gave me a hard look, one eye sleepy. "How did you find this place? As if I didn't know."

"Wes led me right to it."

"Honest, Frank, I didn't kn—"

"Shut up," Frank told him. "And you," he said loudly, looking past my shoulder, "what did I tell you about smoking in here?"

"Sorry, Frank, I forgot." I heard Skinny stamp out his cigarette on the floor.

Frank gave his nephew Carl a crooked smile. "All these chemicals and he forgot."

Carl looked worried. There was a balance scale on the table before him, and he pushed it away as if to disassociate himself from any illegality. Also on the table were a couple dozen Ziploc plastic bags filled with tiny chunks of crystal—maybe ten pounds of ice.

"What are we going to do?" he asked his uncle.

"You mean with Lomax?" Frank looked up at me and grinned. "Gee, I don't know. What do you think we should do with you?"

"Let me take you all into custody," I said.

That got a laugh from Squatty and Frank. Skinny snorted behind me.

"I'm not kidding," I told Frank. "You're finished here. The cops know all about your ice operation and how you're using Butler Manufacturing to ship your product out of state. To Northfield Distributing in Minneapolis, for example."

Frank's face darkened. He swiveled his head to glare at Wes. "Who else have you been blabbing to?"

"No one, Frank, I swear to God."

"For a while I thought you were stealing from the company," I said to Wes. "Then I realized you were taking stuff from the shipment boxes to make room for the bags of ice. Am I right?"

Wes stared at me, frightened.

"How did you—"

"You got a big mouth, Wes," Frank said.

"The cops will be here soon," I put in, trying to make it sound real.

"You son of a bitch," Squatty said to Wes. He pointed his shotgun at him.

Wes stood up hastily, knocking over his chair. He raised his hands, palms forward. "Now wait a minute, take it easy." His voice shook. "I didn't tell him anything. I don't know how he found out any of that."

"I told you we should've never let this asshole in with us, Frank." Squatty had spoken out of the side of his mouth. His eyes and gun were still on Wes. "Let's get rid of him."

"Slow down," Frank said.

Wes backed up, hands still in front of him, shaking as if he were palsied. Squatty walked toward him.

"You fucked up everything."

"No, please, you got this all wrong."

Squatty jacked a shell in the chamber.

"Not in here," Frank said loudly.

Wes bumped into the end of the other table, hard enough to rattle glass beakers. He looked frantically toward the door, but Frank and Carl were on their feet, blocking the exit. Wes edged along the opposite length of the table. "No, please," he begged.

Squatty stepped toward him and raised the shotgun.

"No!"

"Not in here!" Frank yelled.

Too late. Squatty squeezed the trigger, the shotgun boomed, and a microsecond later there was a tremendous flash and concussive shock as vapors in the room ignited and the chemicals on the table exploded, engulfing Squatty and Wes in a ball of fire and slamming me back into Skinny. I caught a glimpse of Carl and Frank stumbling out the door.

I was on my back, on top of Skinny, the shotgun pinned between us.

He tried to shove me off. If it hadn't been for the gun, I would've gladly obliged and gotten the hell out of there,

MICHAEL ALLEGRETTO

because the room—at least the other half of it—was roaring with fire. It howled and crackled and clawed its way toward us along the floor and walls, breathing out acrid smoke.

I gave Skinny an elbow in the face, then quickly rolled over and got my hands on the shotgun. He fought me for it. We tumbled back and forth, first me on top, then him, the gun between us, parallel to our bodies, muzzle pointing up. We were both starting to choke, and I could feel the heat as the fire crept toward us. My hip struck the solid lump of my Magnum tucked in Skinny's belt, and I considered letting go of the shotgun and going for the pistol. But there was no time; his finger was on the trigger, and the muzzle was under my chin. I shoved the barrel away from me just as he jerked his finger.

The front of his head erupted in a burst of blood and flesh, stinging my face with powder and bits of bone.

I yanked the Magnum from his belt and bolted toward the doorway, my arm covering my face, the fire biting my skin. An explosion threw a fireball after me, blowing me across the hallway into the wall. I scrambled to my feet, stumbled down the hallway and out the back exit.

Frank and Carl were already in Frank's T-Bird. But the car was hemmed in between the pickup and Wes's Nissan.

Frank raced the engine, threw it in reverse, and slammed into the Nissan, shoving it back, nearly out of his way. Now the T-Bird jumped forward, banging into the truck.

"Hold it!" I pointed the Magnum at the windshield.

Frank's arm came out the driver's side window, fist filled with an automatic. I didn't wait for him to fire, but squeezed off all six rounds, spattering his end of the windshield with spiderwebbed holes. The T-Bird lurched back into the Nissan, chugged once, and died. Frank's arm hung out the window, limp.

228

The passenger door flew open, and Carl jumped out, face chalk white, hands in the air.

"I give up! Don't shoot!"

"Move it," I told him, waving my empty gun toward the faraway gate.

We gave the building a wide berth. Flames leapt from the windows, and old wood and plaster crackled inside. I pushed Carl down the dark road to the Ford. I put him in the backseat, cuffed his right wrist to his left ankle, then drove to My Brother's Bar.

It was pretty crowded, but people got out of my way as I walked to the back. I called the cops from the pay phone, then found an empty stool at the bar.

The bartender was the same one who'd served me last Monday. He stared at me wide-eyed, possibly because my hair and clothes were scorched and Skinny's brains were drying on my face.

"Jesus, you again? Did you get in another accident?"

"More or less. You got any whiskey back there?"

CHAPTER

34

CARL DYKSTRA WAS EAGER to talk to the cops. There were murder charges hanging in the air, and he didn't want one dropping on him.

His uncle Frank, he said, had lured him into a life of crime, recruiting him right out of college to be a cooker of meth, then ice. They'd begun in California, but after Frank had shot three competitors to death, they'd been forced to move, landing in Denver. For protection Frank brought along muscle—William Royce. He also hired local talent, Skinny and Squatty, whose real names were Terrance Everett and Eugene Styres.

As for Wes Hartman, he'd done more than "smoke ice once in California," as he'd admitted to me; he'd pushed drugs for Frank in Los Angeles. Two years ago, Wes had fled the Coast, frightened by threats from the Korean drug dealers. After spending a few months each in Minneapolis, Kansas City, and Omaha, he'd finally come to Denver. He'd met and married Nicole, whom he saw as a soft touch, a rich man's daughter. The problem was that her father wasn't soft. So Wes looked elsewhere for easy money.

When Frank showed up in Denver, he and Wes reunited. They conspired to produce ice locally and ship it to dealers in other states, places where ice was not yet being manufactured. When a dealer wanted ice, he'd order mugs or other cheap merchandise from Butler Manufacturing. Wes would pack the ice with the mugs, and off the shipment would go.

Wes was careful not to arouse the suspicions of anyone at the company, especially Samuel and Kenneth. Of course Samuel spent more time entertaining his young wife, Clare, than taking care of business. And Kenneth, who was supposed to be in charge, seemed too preoccupied with a scam of his own to notice anything suspicious about shipments to new customers. After a while, Wes's biggest worry was that Samuel would start spending more time at work and less time with Clare.

Then a private eye showed up—Gil Lucero. His questions were upsetting Kenneth, which in turn upset Wes and Frank. They didn't want the status quo disturbed. So Frank and his men took care of Lucero.

And then Samuel was arrested for Clare's murder.

Wes and Frank saw this as a great opportunity. Frank took steps to ensure that Butler would be convicted and out of the way forever. He and his men murdered the key defense witness, Winks Armbruster, and "discouraged" the new private investigator, Jacob Lomax.

The cops asked Carl if Frank had ordered the murder of Clare Butler.

"No," Carl said. "None of us knew who killed her."

That wasn't quite true. One of them had known.

And I knew.

It was past midnight by the time I got home. My jacket, pants, and shirt were scorched beyond repair, so I stuffed them in the trash. My face didn't look so great, either—singed eyebrows and lightly cooked skin. Although not nearly as cooked as Skinny, Squatty, and Wes Hartman.

I took a shower and went to bed.

I got up early the next morning, ate a light breakfast, and watched the local news on TV. There were some spectacular shots of the ice lab engulfed in flames, with firemen spraying water on it and watching it burn to the ground. The newscaster said there were four fatalities, three of whom had been named by the police: Dykstra, Everett, and Styres. The identity of the fourth man was being withheld pending notification of his next of kin.

I drove to Karen Butler's house.

I parked in back. The side door to the garage was open. Two cars were inside—Nicole's and Karen's. I rummaged through the glove compartment until I found what I was looking for—and something extra. Then I knocked on the back door of the house.

Karen answered, surprised.

"What are you doing back here?"

"Sleuthing."

"Find anything?"

"Clare's murderer."

Karen gave me her impression of the famous Butler scowl and asked, "What do you mean?"

"May I come in?"

She hesitated, then stepped aside and let me into the kitchen.

Nicole was sitting at the table with a big yellow mug of steaming coffee. She wore a pristine white top and faded blue jeans, both a bit too big, probably Karen's. Her face was scrubbed, and her hair was tucked back behind her ears. She smiled at me and said, "Hello."

"How're you feeling today?"

"Rested, thank you." She frowned. "What happened to your face?"

"Cooking accident."

Karen stood behind me and demanded, "What did you mean just now at the door?"

"Do you mind if I have some coffee?"

I filled a mug from the glass pot on the stove, then sat across from Nicole. Karen stood beside the table, waiting.

She folded her arms and looked down at me with annoyance, perhaps anger.

I sipped coffee. It was bitter. "As you know, your father always suspected that Clare was murdered by her lover."

Nicole squirmed in her chair. "Are we going to talk about *that*?"

"Perhaps you and I should go in the other room," Karen said to me, as if her sister were an immature child. Maybe she was.

But I made no move to leave the table. "From the beginning, I was looking for the man Clare had been seeing. And for a while I even thought I knew his name—Jeremy Stone. But that turned out to be something else entirely."

"Do you have a point here?" Karen demanded.

"Yes. You and Clare."

Karen glared at me.

Nicole said, "What do you mean?" She looked up at her sister. "What does he mean, 'you and Clare'?"

"Is your sister aware of your sexual preference?" I asked Karen.

"Of *course* she knows I'm gay. So what. So does Kenneth."

"What about your father?"

She hesitated. "No, I don't think so. I've never told him."

"No one's told him," Nicole said, eyes wide, brows arched. "He'd never accept it. He'd—" Her mouth fell open as it dawned on her. "You . . . and *Clare*?" She waited, hoping for a denial. "Karen?"

Karen leaned heavily against the back of the chair. Then she pulled it away from the table and slumped into it. "I guess it doesn't matter now who knows."

Nicole was shocked. "But . . . but how *could* you? Our father's *wife*."

Anger flashed in Karen's eyes. "She wasn't his wife

when I met her," she said. Her anger faded, and she stared into the middle distance. "It wasn't as if I seduced her. I thought of her as a friend—sweet, vulnerable, and in need. That's why I let her stay in this house." She sighed. "The third night here she came into my room, into my bed. We . . . made love. It was so beautiful, as if we were meant to be together. And I did love her. I thought our relationship would last a long, long time." Her face turned grim. "It lasted one month, until she met our father."

"God, Karen, I had no idea." She reached for her sister's hand. "No wonder you hated her so much."

"Hated?" Karen shook her head. "I loved her. I always hoped we'd . . . get back together. Even Teri understood that. We're fond of each other, but with us it's always been off again, on again. With Clare it was something else, something special."

I took another sip of coffee, then pushed the mug away. "You started seeing her again, didn't you. After she'd married your father."

"Yes," she said quietly. "It began a few months ago. Of course, I couldn't tell anyone about it, least of all my father. He would've been devastated—or else gone berserk. Clare told me she was going to leave him, and I assumed we would be together. But then—" Karen's face set in hard lines. "Later, she told me she wasn't just leaving him, she was going away and never coming back."

"That must've made you angry."

"*Angry?* To finally realize that all she wanted me for was *sex?* To see at last how she'd *used* me?"

"You were angry enough to kill her."

Karen glared at me.

"No," Nicole said, frightened. "You can't blame Karen for that."

"I don't. I blame you."

"Me?" Nicole's fear tightened into nervousness.

"What the hell are you saying?" Karen said loudly.

I kept my eyes on Nicole. "I don't know why you did it, but you're the only one who could've murdered Clare that day."

Nicole shook her head no. Karen opened her mouth as if to speak, then closed it.

"It was squealing tires," I said. "That bothered me from day one."

Nicole continued to shake her head ". . . squealing?"

"A neighbor heard tires screech in Samuel's driveway the day of the murder. But when he looked out his window, there was no car in sight. Where was it? I should've figured it out immediately. The car had already pulled into Samuel's garage."

I removed two garage-door openers from my jacket and set them on the table. "I just took those from the glove compartment in your car, Nicole. One is for your condo, and the other is for your father's house, right?"

She stared at the little plastic boxes as if they might explode.

"A three-car garage with two cars," I said. "You were the last child to move out, and you were the most frequent visitor. It makes sense that Samuel would let you keep the third parking space—and the opener. I also found these." I tossed a pair of driving gloves down beside the openers. "Did you wear them when you killed her? If so, the police lab will probably find traces of Clare's blood."

Nicole looked at me and swallowed. Karen stared at her sister, mouth open, brows knit.

"As I said, I don't know why you killed her, only that you did it. If you were high on ice at the time, you may have a good defense. Oliver Westfall might even be able to keep you out of prison."

Nicole licked her lips. "I need to ask Wes . . ."

"Wes is dead. He was blown up last night in an ice lab." There. The next of kin had been notified.

"Oh, my God," Karen said.

Nicole stared at me, one cheek twitching, sweat forming on her upper lip. "Wes is gone?" Her eyes danced about the kitchen, as if she were looking for him. Or maybe her ice pipe.

"Gone forever. And your father is rotting in jail because of you. You tried to confess last night, but no one wanted to believe you. At least I didn't. I was so sure Clare's murder had to do with Wes and the Dykstras. But it was you, wasn't it?"

She said nothing.

"Why did you kill her?"

She hesitated. When she spoke, her voice was small, like a child's. "I thought she was having an affair with Wes."

"Oh, Nicole," Karen moaned.

"He'd been staying out late at night," Nicole added quickly, defending her suspicions. "Leaving me at home alone. All I did was paint. And smoke ice to help me think. I knew he was seeing someone. Clare. I mean, she *had* come on to him in the past, and right in front of me. And he was spending more and more time away from home. I didn't know until too late that he was meeting with those drug people. Anyway, I went to my father's house to tell Clare to stay away from him. I was angry, more angry than I've ever been in my life. I guess I've always hated her, ever since I had to leave home because she moved in and took over. . . ." Nicole heaved another sigh. "So I went to the house and confronted Clare. And you know what she did? Laughed in my face. She said she'd slept with Wes once and once was enough, because he was a 'bum fuck,' just like my father. She wouldn't stop laughing."

Nicole stared vacantly at her hands.

"I'm not sure what happened then. I started to leave, I was in the garage, and then I was back in the kitchen with the wrench in my hand. Clare was sitting at the table, her back to me. I think she was still laughing. At me. At *all* of us. Even Daddy. She'd taken Daddy away from me, and *she thought it was funny.*"

Nicole looked from Karen to me, seeking understanding. Then she lowered her eyes.

"I don't remember hitting her," she said. "The next thing I knew, I was standing over her, with blood everywhere—on Clare, the table, the floor . . . on me."

She shuddered. "I wiped off the wrench, put it back in the garage, and drove home. I was in a daze, I didn't know what to do. Wes was there. He saw all the blood. He knew. He made me take off all my clothes, and he said he'd burn them. He told me to say nothing, that everyone would think that Clare had surprised a burglar. He gave me more ice to smoke to help clear my mind. I guess it worked. Then they arrested Daddy. . . ."

She looked at Karen with pleading eyes. "I would've told, Karen, honest. Eventually. I would've never let them put Daddy in prison. I love him, more than anyone. You believe me, don't you?"

Tears were spilling down Nicole's cheeks. Karen's, too. She took Nicole's hand in hers.

"Yes, honey, I believe you."

CHAPTER

35

NICOLE BUTLER SURRENDERED HERSELF to the police. With Oliver Westfall at her side, of course. He'd already paved the way by discussing the matter with a judge, who also happened to play bridge once a week with Westfall and his wife.

Nicole was released on bail and placed under the care of shrinks. Charges against her were withheld pending a psychiatric evaluation. I doubted that she'd ever go to prison.

Samuel Butler was released from jail, a free man, but with a troubled mind. His younger daughter had murdered his wife. His elder daughter had slept with her. His son-in-law, now dead, had used his company to distribute drugs. And his son and daughter-in-law had stolen from him.

Butler didn't even flinch, at least on the outside. In fact, the next week he was back at work.

I paid him a visit.

I had to wait for twenty minutes in the outer office with the four busy ladies before Butler had time to see me. He sat like a duke behind his big, scarred desk, waving me into a chair, giving me the notorious Butler scowl. The side door to the companion office was closed, but I could hear someone in there on the phone.

"Is that Kenneth in there?"

"Yes," he said with the finality of a prison warden.

"Back where he belongs, right? Under your eye and your thumb."

Butler huffed. "What do you want here, anyway? I've got a business to run."

"It's about the money Kenneth and Doreen took in the name of Jeremy Stone."

"What about it?"

"How much was it?"

Butler pursed his thick lips. "Twenty-three thousand eight hundred."

"Will Kenneth pay it back?"

"Every penny. Not that it's any of your business."

"What are you going to do with the money?"

"Put it back in the company, what else?"

"The company doesn't need it. You didn't even know it was gone."

He scowled. "What're you getting at?"

"There's a better place for it," I told him.

He listened to my explanation. I figured it was worth a shot; no use having a bad ending for *everyone* involved. Finally, and I must admit surprisingly, he agreed. He wrote out a check and handed it to me.

"Good-bye, Mr. Lomax. And do me a favor. Don't ever come back."

"No problem."

The house looked the same—a dirty white cracker box with a patched roof, faded fake shutters, and yellow-stained rain gutters. The screen door still sagged open on its broken spring. Low TV sounds drifted from inside.

I knocked.

Mrs. Jeremy Stone answered, wearing a faded blue blouse and green slacks. A plastic spray bottle of water was clutched in her left hand, probably from ironing.

"Yes?" Then she recognized me. "Oh. Are you here about Jeremy again?"

"In a way." I handed her the check. "Your husband was used for a time by Butler Manufacturing. This is what he earned."

She stared at the check as if it were money from Mars. "I—I don't understand."

"It's yours," I said.

She looked at me dumbly.

"What am I supposed to do with it?"

I had to smile at that. "Take a vacation. Get your screen door fixed. Whatever you want."

Finally, the confusion—and some of the weariness—left her face. "Is this for real?"

"For real."

She smiled timidly and shook her head. "Since Jeremy's been gone, well, this is about the best thing anyone's ever done for me."

"Good."

Her eyes narrowed, but her smile stayed in place. "Is this what you do for a living?"

"Well . . ."

"You must love your job," she said.

"It has its moments."

240